Was this her hero?

As he moved toward her, she noticed his confident, sort of predatory walk. His head dipped slightly as he looked down to her shoeless foot. "Did you lose your glass slipper, Cinderella?"

"I think I was kidnapped." Was it technically a kidnapping when one's own father was behind it?

"You *think?* Don't you remember?"

Remember? What if she couldn't remember. That would make his life difficult, and she liked the idea of that.

"Who are you?" he asked.

He knew good and well who she was. Okay. That did it. Scaring the stuffing out of a girl then playing dumb was not the way to win a fiancée and influence people. She plastered a confused expression on her face and rubbed her fingertips over her forehead. "I—I can't remember."

He gave her a doubtful look. "You're not going to faint, are you?"

Why not? she thought. She needed a ride; this guy needed a lesson.

She made herself go limp and dropped like a stone.

Dear Reader,

Baby birds are chirping, bees are buzzing and the tulips are beginning to bud. Spring is here, so why not revive the winter-weary romantic in you by reading four brand-new love stories from Silhouette Romance this month.

What's an old soldier to do when a bunch of needy rug rats and a hapless beauty crash his retreat? Fall in love, of course! Follow the antics of this funny little troop in *Major Daddy* (#1710) by Cara Colter.

In *Dylan's Last Dare* (#1711), the latest title in Patricia Thayer's dynamite THE TEXAS BROTHERHOOD miniseries, a cranky cowboy locks horns with his feisty physical therapist and then learns she has a little secret she soon won't be able to hide!

Jordan Bishop wants to dwell in a castle and live happily ever after, but somehow things aren't going as she's planned, in *An Heiress on His Doorstep* (#1712) by Teresa Southwick. This is the final title in Southwick's delightful IF WISHES WERE…miniseries in which three friends have their dreams come true in unexpected ways.

When a bookworm meets her prince and discovers she's a real-life princess, will she be able to make her own happy ending? Find out in *The Secret Princess* (#1713) by Elizabeth Harbison.

Celebrate the new season, feel the love and join in the fun by experiencing each of these lively new love stories from Silhouette Romance!

Mavis C. Allen
Associate Senior Editor

Please address questions and book requests to:
Silhouette Reader Service
U.S.: 3010 Walden Ave., P.O. Box 1325, Buffalo, NY 14269
Canadian: P.O. Box 609, Fort Erie, Ont. L2A 5X3

An Heiress on His Doorstep

TERESA SOUTHWICK

SILHOUETTE *Romance*®

Published by Silhouette Books

America's Publisher of Contemporary Romance

SILHOUETTE BOOKS

ISBN 0-373-19712-8

AN HEIRESS ON HIS DOORSTEP

Visit Silhouette at www.eHarlequin.com

Printed in U.S.A.

Books by Teresa Southwick

Silhouette Romance

Wedding Rings and Baby Things #1209
The Bachelor's Baby #1233
A Vow, a Ring, a Baby Swing #1349
The Way to a Cowboy's Heart #1383
And Then He Kissed Me #1405
With a Little T.L.C. #1421
The Acquired Bride #1474
Secret Ingredient: Love #1495
The Last Marchetti Bachelor #1513
**Crazy for Lovin' You* #1529
**This Kiss* #1541
**If You Don't Know by Now* #1560
**What If We Fall in Love?* #1572
Sky Full of Promise #1624
†*To Catch a Sheik* #1674
†*To Kiss a Sheik* #1686
†*To Wed a Sheik* #1696
††*Baby, Oh Baby!* #1704
††*Flirting with the Boss* #1708
††*An Heiress on His Doorstep* #1712

Silhouette Books

The Fortunes of Texas
Shotgun Vows

Silhouette Special Edition

The Summer House #1510
  "Courting Cassandra"
*Midnight, Moonlight
  & Miracles* #1517

*The Marchetti Family
**Destiny, Texas
†Desert Brides
††If Wishes Were…

TERESA SOUTHWICK

lives in Southern California with her hero husband who is more than happy to share with her the male point of view. An avid fan of romance novels, she is delighted to be living out her dream of writing for Silhouette Books.

The fortune-teller said…

To be a princess and live in a palace—
love is the risk, deception the malice.

If the three born on February twenty-ninth rub
the magic from the lamp and make a wish—
on that day that comes only once every
four years—each shall receive her
most coveted desire.

But there is peril.

Each of the three must see beyond the evident.
Look into the soul of the one her heart
has chosen.
Only then will she find the truth
that is hers alone.

Chapter One

Jordan Bishop said goodbye to terror and went straight to furious. Being kidnapped was *not* the way she'd planned to start her first vacation in two years.

She looked at the guy who'd abducted her. He was hardly more than a kid, an average-looking young man. Average height, average looks and average brown hair. They'd been waiting on this deserted road for what felt like hours, and he'd refused to tell her why. Jordan was fed up.

"I have to go to the bathroom," she said.

He glanced over at her from the driver's seat. "Do you see one, sweetheart?" His voice was rife with sarcasm.

That does it, she thought.

She pressed her legs together. "I wonder how this leather seat would hold up in the event of an unfortunate accident."

That wiped the sarcastic expression off his face. "You gotta go in the bushes."

"Any port in a storm," she replied.

She'd been terrified when he'd grabbed her, expecting to be assaulted or murdered any second. But that feeling faded when he kept driving. After stopping, he hadn't made a single threatening move. It felt like he was waiting for something. And she didn't intend to be around when the wait was over.

He got out of the car and walked around to her side, opening the door with his keys in his hand. He unlocked the cuff hooked to the passenger handhold above her head. The other cuff was attached to her wrist. When he glanced away to put his keys back in his pocket, she swiveled in her seat and kicked out as hard as she could with both legs, making him stumble backward. If she'd known she would be in this mess, she'd have dressed more appropriately. Now was no time to worry about her tight skirt. At least it was short, giving her some maneuverability.

While the creep was getting his footing, Jordan jumped out of the SUV. She winced when a small rock dug into her bare heel. She'd lost one of her pumps when he'd first grabbed her.

He grinned. "Nice try."

"I thought so."

As he started toward her, she braced for her next move. She was about to find out if all those self-defense classes were worth the price. When he put his hands on her upper arms, she jabbed the three-inch spike heel of her remaining pump into his instep. He cried out, but before he could react, she raised her knee and rammed it into his groin. He grunted in pain and doubled over wheezing, then dropped to the ground groaning. This was the part where she was supposed to run like hell.

But where? Even if she knew which way to run, she was out in the sticks, with no sign of civilization in sight. She had to get the keys, but she didn't want to get in too close to him. Even though he was still rolling around and groaning. But how long did it take a man to recover from a knee to the groin?

"Bishop's not paying me enough for this," he muttered to himself.

Bishop? He couldn't have said what she thought she'd heard. "What did you say? Who's paying you?" she demanded.

He glared at her. "Your father."

"My *father?* I don't believe you."

"I couldn't make up something this weird," he said, sitting up. "He hired me to kidnap you."

"Why?"

"It's a setup. To find you a man."

"You?" she asked, shocked.

"No. And I resent your implication and your tone."

She didn't give a rat's behind what he resented. "Look, buster, my patience is wearing thin. You scared me out of my wits, you handcuffed me." She held up her wrist with the dangling metal still attached. "And you made me lose my shoe. It was my favorite pair and very expensive."

"You're an heiress. You can afford it. Bill your father."

"That's not the point. And none of your business. Start talking. I want the facts, from the beginning."

He held his head in his hands. "Your father has the perfect guy for you. Sir Galahad is due here any minute to waltz in for the rescue. You know, be your hero.

After that you're supposed to fall for him and get married. Happy ever after and all that crap. It's the truth. I swear.''

"I don't believe this," she said, throwing up her hands.

But the statement was rhetorical, because the more she thought about it, the more she did believe him. It would certainly explain why her father had been so insistent that she have lunch with him today. The kidnapper knew where to find her because her father had set her up. "So when was this guy supposed to be here?"

"An hour ago."

"Figures. Apparently Daddy picks heroes as well as he picks kidnappers.''

"It's my first kidnapping and not my sphere of expertise," he said defensively.

"So where did my father find you? Thugs-R-Us?"

"Very funny. I work part-time at Bishop, Inc. while I go to college.''

He wasn't very tall, about five-six or five-seven to her five foot one. But he was beefy. If he hadn't surprised her when she'd been leaving her father's office, her self-defense moves would have been more effective. They wouldn't have been effective just now if he'd been a professional kidnapper. Why had he done it?

"Did you need the money? Is that why you agreed to this ridiculous Machiavellian farce?''

"I bet you think I don't know what that means." He looked up at her, his eyes narrowed. "It's hard to say no to your father. And he's my boss.''

"You should get another boss." She couldn't get another father.

''No kidding.''

She tried not to feel sorry for him, but he really did look pathetic sitting in the dirt at the side of the road. Speaking of which, she hadn't seen another car come along the whole time they'd been here. What the heck was her father thinking? Rage expanded inside her.

''So who's the tardy Prince Charming my father is trying to hook me up with this time?''

''Didn't get his name.''

''And no way to contact him,'' she guessed.

''Nope.''

She was twenty-four-and-a-half years old. Her father had pretty much ignored her for the first twenty-four. But he'd changed in the last six months. Right after his heart attack when she'd been in New Orleans for her birthday. A near-death experience gives you a different perspective he'd said. From her perspective, he was acting just plain weird. His explanation was that he wouldn't be around forever, and he wanted to see her settled and secure before he kicked the bucket.

At first she'd thought the change was really sweet and had high hopes of finally building a relationship with him. But he'd gone after this the way he'd built his business—with single-minded determination. He'd started small, with a casual introduction to a man of his choice, then dinner for three, then dinner for three where only she and the man showed up. Then a weekend away for her and her dad. But dad had been conspicuously absent. It was just her and Harman Bishop's current front-runner for her affections.

And the problem was escalating. Last week he'd given Clark Caldwell, a guy she'd broken up with, the key to her apartment to arrange a romantic dinner for two. Her dad wasn't the subtle type. Damn the torpedoes, full speed ahead. Another day, another guy. No regard for consequences or whom he steamrolled. He'd been butting into her life no matter how often or how vehemently she told him to stop.

But this was the last straw. How stupid did he think she was? And what kind of clown was he trying to set her up with? What kind of man would go along with this? Scratch that. She *so* didn't want to know.

The guy groaned as he stood up, then without warning grabbed her. "Okay. Back in the car."

"No way," she said, pulling hard to try and free her arm.

"I gotta take you back to your dad."

The thought of the man who'd set this series of events in motion generated a red-hot haze of fury. She grabbed his right ear and yanked.

"Ow," he cried, dropping his hand from her arm. "Look, lady," he pleaded, "I only got half the money. If I don't—"

"Tell it to someone who cares." In a strictly reflex action, she raised her knee again.

"Okay, okay, you win."

She backed away and looked around. They were on a farm-to-market road somewhere in Texas, and she couldn't be more specific because this idiot had driven her around for hours. On either side of the two-lane road, rolling hills stretched as far as the eye could see. No stores, no houses, no phones. And she'd dropped her purse with the cell phone inside when she'd been abducted.

Behind her she heard her father's lackey mutter something like "not enough money in the world to put up with this crap." No kidding. When she got ahold of her father, she was going to give him a piece of her mind. Of course, she'd done that many times in the past, and still he'd pulled a stunt like this. She had to think of some way to stop him, to convince him not to interfere in her life.

She took a step, and a pebble bit into her heel again. "Ouch," she said, looking down.

Then she heard the SUV engine roar to life. Spinning around, she watched the big tires throw up dirt and rocks as it screeched onto the road.

The car stopped beside her. "Your hero should be here any minute." Then the window went up, and her abductor drove away.

At first she was too stunned to move. Then she was too angry to think straight.

"That damn thug-in-training should be grounded for the rest of his natural born days," she ranted, limping in a circle.

"Harman Bishop is going to rue the day he messed with me," she sputtered. "An accident of DNA does not give him carte blanche to commandeer my life."

Jordan stood by the side of the road, one shoe off, one shoe on, the handcuff still dangling from her wrist. She looked toward the west. She knew it was west because the sun was descending in the sky and would soon disappear behind the rolling hills on the horizon. In the distance, she saw a car coming from the direction her kidnapper had gone. Was this her hero?

The vehicle, a very pricey luxury model, stopped in front of her. The door opened, and a man got out. He was tall, muscular and looked to be in his early thirties, just exactly the age her father would have chosen. As he moved toward her she noticed his confident, sort of predatory walk. She noticed he was late, too.

When he stopped in front of her, she saw that his

eyes were hidden behind aviator sunglasses. His head dipped slightly as he looked down to her shoeless foot. "Did you lose your glass slipper, Cinderella?"

So Mr. Wonderful was playing dumb. "Are you my prince here to see if the shoe fits?"

"I'm here to see if you need help. Car trouble?"

"Not exactly."

He frowned as he looked around the empty road. "How *did* you get here?"

She started to raise her arm, and the handcuff jangled at the end of her wrist. "I—I think I was kidnapped," she said.

Was it technically a kidnapping when one's own father was behind it? How could he do this to her? And how could this guy go along with it? What was in it for him? Most people sent a card when they wanted to reach out and touch someone. Her father picked a hell of a way to say he cared. And did he really? He hadn't even hired a competent kidnapper. He got an amateur, a guy she could take with weeny moves, and now *this* winner. Men, she thought disgusted.

He continued to stare at her when she didn't answer right away. "You think you were kidnapped? That's a new one," he mumbled. "Don't you remember?"

Remember? He was taking the playing dumb thing to a new high, or low as the case may be. What if she couldn't remember? That would make his life difficult, and she liked the idea of that. She embraced the saying "When life gives you lemons, make lemonade." What if she gave this bozo enough lemonade to drown in?

"Who are you?" he asked.

He knew good and well who she was. Okay. That did it. Scaring the stuffing out of a girl then playing dumb was *not* the way to win a fiancée and influence people. She was going to make this as difficult as possible for him. She plastered a confused expression on her face, and it didn't require Drama 101 to pull it off. She really was confused by the events of the past few hours.

With the handcuff dangling in front of her, she rubbed her fingertips over her forehead. ''I—I can't remember.''

He gave her a doubtful look. ''You're not going to faint, are you?''

Why not? she thought. She needed a ride; this guy needed a lesson. She made herself go limp and dropped like a stone.

Chapter Two

J. P. Patterson automatically reached out and caught the woman against him. As he lifted her limp body into his arms, her head settled onto his shoulder and he studied her face. It was fine-boned and lovely, with smooth, soft-looking skin. And she was heavier than she looked, which he attributed to muscle, because her pencil-thin skirt wouldn't hide any fat.

Nine out of ten guys would be grateful this woman had fallen into their arms. Apparently J.P. was number ten because he wished she'd fainted in front of the other nine guys. This beautiful brunette had *scam* written all over her. He didn't for a minute believe this act and cursed the fact that he couldn't just let her hit the pavement. But he had no illusions about trying to get the truth out of her.

He had to give her credit. This scheme was definitely more elaborate and imaginative than the ever-popular sneaking into his hotel room and waiting naked in his bed. The dangling handcuff, the missing shoe and being stranded in the middle of nowhere were all nice touches. Her mission to meet him had been planned and executed with the precision of a military invasion. And that wasn't ego talking. It was the voice of experience.

He didn't flatter himself that women fell all over him because of his sex appeal and animal magnetism. The only magnet was his fortune. He'd made *People* magazine's list of the fifty most beautiful people— Sexiest Gazillionaire it read under his picture. Again, nine out of ten men would be flattered. To him, it was simply more publicity he didn't want or need.

Women threw themselves at him on a fairly regular basis. Just like this one in his arms. The question was, now what did he do with her?

This was the road to his house. It seemed obvious she'd had someone drop her off here so she could wait for him to come by, knowing he wouldn't be able to leave her. He thought about setting her on the blacktop to see how fast the faint would last. He could simply drive away. Unfortunately, his mother had raised him to be a gentleman. He turned toward his SUV and managed to open the passenger door and get her inside.

He looked over his shoulder in the direction of town. He'd just come from there; the sheriff was there. Turning her over to the sheriff would be his best option. But it was a long drive and the estate was closer. Besides, his mother had just arrived for a visit, and she was waiting. He belted the stranger in and went around the front of the car, then entered the driver's side.

He drove to the estate in a couple of minutes. Again he thought how precisely she'd planned her campaign as he braked in front of the closed security gates. He pressed the button on his remote control and the gates opened wide. He guided the vehicle up the long, tree-lined drive, then parked in the semicircular area in front of the house. Turning off the ignition, he glanced at the woman in the other seat.

She opened her eyes—big, beautiful brown eyes, he noticed—and sat up. How convenient.

"Where am I?"

Classic question and certainly in character for the part she was playing. But he was sure she knew exactly where she was. He could end her game any time, but he wanted to wait. It would give him a certain satisfaction to watch her reaction when she tripped up and the plan imploded. And she *would* trip up. He was certain of that, too.

"This is my home," he said, opening his door. "I brought you here to call the sheriff and report the kidnapping." He watched her closely.

"I can't wait."

A cool customer. Detail noted. He got out of the car and went to her side to swing the door wide. She slid out and her skirt rode up, revealing a flash of shapely thigh. A calculated move, like baiting a hook. He didn't plan to be her unsuspecting mackerel. But he had to admit, if there was any silver lining to the situation, this view of tempting, tanned flesh was it. Then she was standing on the concrete driveway, wob-bling because she was wearing only one high heel.

"You might want to take your shoe off," he sug-gested, pointing to her foot.

A dainty foot, he noted. And her nylons were in shreds. That short Band-Aid of a skirt didn't hide much of her legs and her thighs were pretty spectacular, too, even in the tattered panty hose.

To steady herself, she touched his arm. Her hand was small and warm against his skin, and his pulse spiked once before he drew in a deep breath to stabilize it.

She slipped off her high heel then straightened and looked it over as if she'd never seen it before. "Looks like real leather."

"It does," he agreed. "You apparently have a memory of genuine leather."

"Apparently I do. Along with exceptionally good taste in footwear." She shook her head. "I like this shoe, and I wish I knew where the other one was."

The comment seemed sincere, but he would bet she wasn't all that worried. Her accomplice was probably taking good care of it. "Let's go inside."

She turned and froze. Her jaw dropped as she silently stared for several long moments at his house. Either she'd really fainted, which he doubted, or she hadn't peeked on the way up the drive to preserve the pretense that she'd passed out. Either way, her surprise seemed genuine.

"Good Lord, it looks like a castle. Turrets and towers and stones, oh my."

"It is a castle. Very famous in this part of Texas. In fact that's how the town of Castle Rock got its name."

She rubbed her forehead. "I don't remember if I've ever heard of it."

He studied her, again waiting for a slip in her facade. A weakness in her expression. He found none. Not surprising since the rest of this operation had been planned so precisely and in such a detailed manner.

He couldn't believe her research hadn't included information about where he lived, so he had to assume her apparent shock meant she was a very good actress.

Then he looked at the impressive stone walls surrounding the extensive manicured grounds of the estate. He studied the main entrance to the house, stately and towering above them. The sheer majesty of the building was something he always took for granted, along with the heavy double doors that led inside.

But he tried to put himself in her shoes, so to speak, he thought, glancing at her bare feet. He lived in the country on five acres and the security surrounding him was state of the art. If she'd been casing the place, he would know. That meant she probably hadn't seen it in person. Up close, it must look pretty extraordinary.

He'd always thought so. "In the late 1800s, my family made more money in cattle than they knew what to do with. Someone on my mother's side decided to buy an English castle. They took it apart and reassembled it here in Texas brick by brick."

"That must have cost enough to feed a third world country for a year."

"Probably." He was volunteering a lot of information to someone who was trying to con him and could only chalk it up to pride in the family digs. Besides, he figured she'd done her homework and already knew the details. "We call it Patterson palace."

"A palace," she said, an odd expression on her face. Then she met his gaze. "Patterson? Is that your name?"

As if she didn't know. "J. P. Patterson. And you are?"

"I wish I knew." She shifted her bare feet and winced, then brushed the bottom of one bare foot across the top of the other. "Ouch. You wouldn't think a palace would allow pebbles."

"It's not Camelot," he said wryly. "Let's go inside. My mother's waiting."

Her gaze narrowed as she looked up at him. "She is?"

"Yes." He didn't like the look on her face. "What's wrong?"

"There's just something about a guy in his thirties who lives with his mother."

"Without a memory, you know this—how?"

"Instinct. Just an impression. I can't explain it." She shrugged. "If it's all the same to you, maybe I'll just take my chances back on the road."

Her implication irritated him, and he felt compelled to defend himself. "My mother lives in a condo in Dallas. She's here to visit."

"If you say so. And since we're here, I can call the sheriff. Like you said. I'd appreciate the use of your telephone."

"After you," he said, holding out his hand.

With an air of stubbornness, she lifted her chin and preceded him up the four steps to the entrance. When she stopped at the door, he reached around her and opened it.

She halted in the entryway, staring from side to side, then up at the ornately carved stone ceiling. "Wow."

"This way," he said. "Mother's probably in the great room."

Pride in the family digs took him only so far, and he was done now. The sooner he got the sheriff out here to deal with this faker the better.

They moved past the front rooms used as a parlor and living room and headed toward the kitchen and

great room, which looked out over the rear gardens
and a pool with a brick patio.

"J.P.? Is that you?"

"Yes, Mother."

They walked into the huge room where his mother
sat in an overstuffed chair beside the stone fireplace
taking up one full wall. J.P. could almost stand up
straight in it. They'd always joked that their ancestors
probably used it to roast a steer on a spit.

Audrey put aside the book she'd been reading and
looked up. When she spotted his companion, she
frowned. "Good lord, J.P., what have you done to that
young woman?"

"Nothing. I rescued her." He glanced at the companion in question and was sure he saw her glare at
him. But the look disappeared so fast he wasn't certain. "She was stranded at the side of the road and
there was no car in sight. That seemed odd, so I
stopped."

His mother closed her book and stood, then went to
meet them. She was taller than the gold-digging
stranger. "What's your name, dear?"

"I—I don't remember."

"J.P.?"

"All she told me is that she thought she'd been
kidnapped," he said.

His mother lifted the dangling handcuff and studied
the shoeless stranger, frowning as she took in every
detail of her disheveled appearance. "Good heavens.
How did you get free?"

Mystery woman shook her head. "My last clear
memory is standing on the side of the road and a car
driving away. Fast. Then your son stopped to help me.
I'm afraid I was so overwhelmed I fainted."

His mother slid her arm around the faker's shoulders and led her to the couch on the long oak-panelled wall. He wanted to warn his mother of his suspicions, but didn't want to make a scene. It wasn't worth the aggravation since the sheriff would deal with the situation soon enough.

"Poor dear," his mother said. "Is there anyone we can call who might be worried about you?"

"I can't remember."

"J.P., did you find a purse or anything that might give us a clue to her identity?"

"I didn't look," he said.

"For goodness' sake, that's basic investigative technique."

"She passed out, Mother. I had my hands full."

"Sorry, dear. Of course you couldn't let her fall."

If there was any plus for him in this whole situation, it had been holding her in his arms. She was soft and curvy in all the right places. He was a guy, and he'd noticed.

"I'm Audrey Patterson," his mother said. "Obviously you met my son."

"My hero."

Was there the slightest trace of sarcasm in the stranger's tone? When his gaze locked with hers, the hostility there was quickly replaced by innocence and a fragile victim expression.

"Think, dear," his mother said to her. "Can you tell us where you live? Maybe where you work?"

She was working right now, J.P. thought. Playing his mother like a violin.

"I can't remember anything."

"Should we take you to the emergency room? Perhaps a doctor should check you over?"

"My head doesn't hurt, and I don't feel any bumps or bruises. I don't hurt anywhere, in fact. But my memory is blank." She looked appropriately pathetic.

Audrey patted her hand. "It must be amnesia caused by emotional trauma."

Not yet, J.P. thought. But soon. With the sheriff's help, he planned to give her a healthy dose of trauma.

"Mother, I brought her here to call the sheriff."

"That's right," the stranger agreed. "If you'll tell me where your phone is, I'll do that. The sooner the sheriff gets involved, the better." She met his gaze, and her own narrowed. This time there was no doubt about the animosity. "I don't want the kidnapper's trail to get cold. Or any accomplices to get away."

What was that all about? She was playing this to the hilt. And the way she was looking at him. If he didn't know better, he'd swear she was accusing him of something.

"What are you implying?" he asked sharply.

"J.P., your tone," his mother admonished. "She's been through a terrible ordeal. You'd be hostile too if you couldn't remember your name."

"If I didn't know my name, I'd be trying everything possible to remember."

"It's not good to force the memories," Audrey said.

"And you know this—how?" he asked.

"It happens that way in all the romance novels," she said defensively. "And the movies. They always say the victim needs to rest and feel secure. With relaxation, the memories will start to come back. Probably in isolated flashes."

"Well, I bet the sheriff can make her feel safe and secure. I'll just go make a phone call and get him out here."

"You're my hero," their guest said again. "Coming to my rescue yet again."

He looked at her, pure and pretty as she sat in the circle of Audrey's maternal embrace. Victimizing him was one thing; he was used to it. But he wanted to shield his mother from the gold diggers who were only after his money. The last time he'd let his guard down, he'd been hammered by a woman with the face of an angel and the soul of a snake.

"I'll be back in a minute," he said.

Jordan watched J.P. walk out of the room and breathed a sigh of relief. She looked at the blond, blue-eyed older woman beside her and wondered if she knew her son was an underhanded weasel.

A weasel who wasn't hard on the eyes. In the looks department, J. P. Patterson was a twelve on a scale of one to ten. She'd always had a weakness for dark-haired, blue-eyed men. But her father couldn't have known that because he hardly knew her at all. At least he'd picked a hunk to be her hero. A hunk with money, judging by where he lived.

She hadn't gotten a good look at this place until she'd slid out of the car. It was a real, honest-to-goodness castle with a drawbridge over a moat and everything. It was like Sleeping Beauty's castle at Disneyland—only bigger. And with real rooms, not a facade. Really big rooms with beveled, leaded glass windows covered by velvet drapes with gold-braided tiebacks. It was unbelievable.

The first thing she'd thought of was her leap year birthday in New Orleans when she and her friends had rubbed the lamp and made their wishes. Hers had been to be a princess and live in a palace.

She'd been joking, but apparently fate had a sense

of humor. If this guy lived here, no way on God's green earth would she live here with him. He was an underhanded scoundrel, a willing and eager participant in this outrageous kidnapping scheme of her father's.

Audrey Patterson patted her hand again. "Can I get you something to drink, dear? Water? Something stronger?"

"No, thanks."

She would have something stronger after the sheriff got there. Then it would be time to celebrate giving J.P. back a little of his own medicine. She just didn't want to do it in front of this woman who seemed a decent sort. If she didn't already know what a conniver her son was, Jordan didn't want to rub her nose in it. Although she did wonder why he was so eager to call the sheriff. Could be he thought he was in the clear. That there was nothing to tie him to the scheme.

Except her father.

Anger knotted inside her. Somehow she had to teach Harman Bishop to mind his own business. Show him he couldn't make up for twenty-four years of indifference with six months of meddling.

J.P. walked back into the room and his mother said, "What did the sheriff say? When can we expect him?"

"Tomorrow morning."

"What?" Jordan asked, surprised.

He looked at her. "It's a small town. The sheriff's department reflects that. On Friday night its resources are stretched to the limit. And this isn't an emergency."

"Since when is a kidnapping not an emergency? I agree with—" Audrey hesitated, obviously not knowing what to call Jordan "—our guest, that we don't want the kidnapper's trail to get cold."

"I'm not so sure there's any trail to cool off," he said.

Jordan thought there was the hint of derision and a shade of cynicism in his voice. Or maybe it was just guilt.

"No one can come out until morning?" she asked.

"That's what he said." He slid his hands into the pockets of his khakis. The long sleeves of his yellow shirt were rolled to just below the elbows. It was a good look.

"That's unacceptable," his mother commented. "When I see Sheriff Michaels, I intend to give him a piece of my mind."

"I actually talked to Rick. He's out on a call, but he said since the victim is physically all right, we should sit tight and someone will be out tomorrow to take a statement." He looked at Jordan. "Or I could drive her into town and leave her at the station."

Jordan stood. "Then that's probably the best thing to do."

"Absolutely not," Audrey said.

"But, Mom, the department has resources—"

Audrey shook her head. "Not the kind she needs. That institutional, bureaucratic little office won't give her the feeling of safety and security necessary for her memory to return."

"You're very kind, Mrs. Patterson," Jordan said. "I've burdened *you* enough already." But she hadn't burdened him nearly enough, she thought, meeting J.P.'s narrowed gaze.

"Nonsense, dear. Frankly, I was wondering how I was going to keep myself entertained. My condo is being painted, and J.P. insisted I stay with him while the work is being done.''

How about that? The man was nice to his mother. But even serial killers had redeeming qualities, and she wanted her pound of flesh for what Harman Bishop and J. P. Patterson had put her through.

''Mom, if she wants to go, I'll be happy to take her into town.''

''Really, J.P., you rescued this young woman only to dispose of her at the sheriff's office? She called you her hero. That doesn't seem especially heroic to me.'' She looked at Jordan. ''My dear, you can't remember who you are or where you live. Rick Michaels is an exceptional sheriff in the finest tradition of Texas lawmen. But, as with most men, he has the sensitivity of a gnat. You're concerned about putting us out and that's very sweet. But this place is big enough to put up several professional sports teams. I think we can handle you for one night. Maybe by morning you'll have your memory back.''

Jordan glanced at J.P. who looked as if he would rather eat glass than have her stay. He was good. What an act. Academy Award material. And it made her furious. She'd been put out and put upon with this farce. Surely there was some law against staging a kidnapping. He'd portrayed the rescuer, but he was part of this conspiracy. She'd wanted to make a statement; she'd hoped to embarrass him in front of the sheriff. She'd been frightened to death and held captive by a wimpy little twit who caved at the first sign of trouble. And J. P. Patterson had gone along with the manipulation. What kind of man would do a thing like that?

She wanted to beat him at his own game; she

wanted it bad. Sticking around until tomorrow would give her an opportunity.

"Thank you, Mrs. Patterson. I'd be happy and very relieved to accept your generosity."

Chapter Three

J.P. studied the slender wrist with the handcuff attached. Audrey had suggested he figure out a way to remove it while she found some clean clothes for their guest.

The stranger looked around the room. "Nice kitchen. Lots of counter space with that island in the center. The granite countertops are really beautiful. The different shades of brown and beige are a nice complement to the floor tile."

"I'm glad you approve."

"And this," she said, studying the oak table and eight chairs set in the bay area. "This looks like an antique. Did it come with the house?"

"It's old. It belonged to my great-great-grandmother."

"It's in wonderful shape," she said, rubbing her hand over the wood surface. The cuff scraped against the edge and she quickly grabbed it. "Sorry. I'll be glad to get rid of this."

He picked up the bolt cutters he'd found in the tool-shed. "Okay, give me your hand."

"I'm going to pray you didn't mean that the way it sounded." Big, beautiful brown eyes stared at the large tool in his hand. "You're not going to cut off my hand with that, are you?"

His gaze lowered to the button on her silk blouse that held the material together over her firm breasts. "I'm going to cut off the cuff, unless you've got a key tucked away somewhere."

The idea of fishing for it sent a shaft of heat straight to his groin. He didn't trust her as far as he could throw her, but, unfortunately, that didn't shut down his appreciation of her attributes.

"Regrettably, when the kidnapper pealed rubber on the highway as he drove off, he didn't toss me the key."

"A simple no would suffice."

"We'd all like things we can't have. For instance," she said, "I'd like whoever's behind this kidnapping in these cuffs."

"Me, too." He met her gaze and waited for her to blink. She didn't.

"He probably didn't pull it off by himself," she said, with what seemed like studied casualness.

"I came to the same conclusion."

"Really? How about that? We agree on something."

He was just sliding the bolt cutters beneath the circle of metal on her delicate wrist when he looked up and saw her smile. He was struck by the fact that she was quite remarkably beautiful. As those shock waves hit him, his hand slipped.

She snatched hers back. "Are you sure you know

what you're doing with those things? One of us could get hurt.''

''This isn't rocket science,'' he snapped, annoyed with himself for the lapse.

''Neither is kidnapping. What do you suppose the penalty is for abducting someone against their will?''

''Penalty?''

''Yeah, as in it's against the law. And when a person breaks the law, there's a cost for it. Like jail time,'' she added.

''I suppose so.''

''And what about accomplices? Coconspirators?''

What the hell was she doing? Was it like hiding in plain sight? Throw him off her trail by discussing the transgression? ''What about them?''

''Do you think the punishment for a crime is as stiff for the brawn as it is for the brains behind it?'' she asked sweetly.

''I have no idea. What do you think?''

''I think everyone involved should pay big time.''

''Me, too.'' He let out a breath and started attempt number two to slide the bolt cutters beneath the circle on her arm. This time he didn't make the mistake of looking at her.

''So you think jail time is appropriate?''

He kept his eyes on the metal. ''Whoever hatched a kidnapping scheme to swindle money and anyone who goes along with said scheme should be locked up. And the key thrown away.''

The cuff was closed as far as it would go, but her wrist was so slender he easily had enough room to get the jaws of the tool between the metal and her flesh. The inside of her arm was pale, a stark contrast to the tan on her forearm. Her skin looked soft, smooth. He lined up the blades of the cutter very carefully. In spite of her sneaky actions, he had no desire to hurt her. Then he pressed the handles of the bolt cutter together and felt the stiff resistance. This wasn't going to be like a hot knife through butter.

"Do you think those things would cut through the bars of a jail cell?" she asked.

"No." What was it with her and retribution? She was the one flirting with a felony. But if he confronted her, she'd only deny it. No point in wasting his breath.

However, he wished big time that the scent of her skin didn't remind him so much of twisted sheets, temptation and sin. The perfume she was wearing smelled subtle, expensive. A tool of her trade as surely as the one he was using.

"Hold still," he warned, exerting more pressure on the bolt-cutter's handles.

"Like I would make a sudden move when you've got the jaws of death on my arm." She watched his progress in silence for several moments. "It occurs to me that if a felon has enough money, he can hire some high-powered legal counsel."

"What does that mean?"

"It seemed an obvious statement of fact to me. There are stories in the news all the time about crooks who get off after hiring pricey legal eagles."

"I'll take your word for it."

She glanced around the large kitchen. "I'd say you have a few bucks."

"You think?" he asked. She knew darn good and well he did. "What was your first clue?"

He pressed the handles together with as much force as he dared and felt the blades come together as they cut completely through the metal. He put down the tool, then worked the cuff off her wrist.

"Paupers don't live in palaces," she pointed out, meeting his gaze.

"No, princesses do."

She looked startled for a moment, but recovered quickly. "Are you looking for a princess?"

"No." Heaven forbid.

"Good thing." She rubbed her wrist, now free of the handcuff. "But if you change your mind, you might try adding diamonds to that bracelet before you put it on a girl's wrist next time."

He stared at her, surprised at her boldness. "I didn't put that bracelet on this time. The kidnapper did." He studied the gleam in her eyes, the rebellious lift of her chin. "For a woman who's been recently traumatized, you seem to be taking it all in stride."

"I suppose the silver lining of amnesia is that you can't remember trauma. It's the mind's way of protecting itself," she said calmly.

"It just seems to me that someone who's gone through a kidnapping then lost her memory over the whole thing would be more shaken up from the experience. You seem to be handling it very well. Pretty scrappy."

She shrugged. "What can I say? I'm a scrappy sort of gal."

"Is that a memory returning?"

"No. Probably just my natural personality coming out. Trauma may have stolen my memories, but it won't keep me down." She stood and touched the twisted metal he'd just removed from her wrist. "Next time remember diamonds are a girl's best friend."

He opened his mouth to retort when his mother walked into the room.

"How's it going?" she asked.

"Mission accomplished," the mystery woman said, holding up her now naked wrist.

Audrey stood beside him. "I've been thinking."

"That's a dangerous prospect," he said.

"Don't be disrespectful, J.P. I brought you into this world. I can take you out."

"Yes, Mother." He thought it wise to hide his grin.

"As I was saying, we can't keep calling our guest 'hey, you.' Until you remember your name," she said to the woman, "I think we should call you Jane Doe."

"Don't tell me," he said. "That's what all the books and movies do."

Audrey shrugged. "Well, it is."

"Jane works for me," said the mystery woman.

"Good." Audrey nodded with satisfaction. "J.P., why don't you show Jane upstairs to the window seat room. I think you'll be comfortable there, dear. You can clean up. Everything you'll need is there, and I've left some clean clothes on the bed. You'll probably want to rest so I'll send up a light supper for you."

"Please don't go to any trouble on my account," Jane said, absently rubbing her wrist. Or was it nerves making her do that?

"It's no trouble. I want you to relax and feel safe."

"You're very kind," Jane said.

J.P. moved toward the kitchen doorway. "Follow me."

He thought about blowing her cover, pointing out the flaws in her plan. Then he figured there was no point in a confrontation since she would be gone by morning. And he wouldn't upset his mother. But

"Jane's" comments about princesses, palaces and precious stones proved that she was no different from all the other women who had gone to great lengths to meet him.

It wasn't him she was after him. It was all about his money.

The next morning Jordan left her lovely room. Audrey was right. She'd been very comfortable tucked away there, although she'd felt like the princess in *The Princess and the Pea,* in a bed that seemed as if it was several stories off the ground. She'd had to climb a wooden step stool to get in it. But the velvet curtains at the beveled-glass windows, heavy, carved cherry-wood furniture, gold fixtures in the attached bath—it was all very wonderful.

She marveled at the rest of the house as she came downstairs. It made her interior decorator's heart beat a little faster. The graceful arches and stained-glass windows high in the brick walls were spectacular. Twin oak staircases curved from the main floor to the second story. Reverently, she touched the bannister as she descended. Then she used it for real to keep from tripping. Audrey had loaned her a T-shirt and sweatpants that were too long. If she wasn't careful, she'd go down the hard way. How would J.P. explain her broken neck to her father?

There was a certain irony in the fact that her father was throwing her at J. P. Patterson, a man who lived in a castle. She'd become an interior decorator over her father's protests. Now, she would give her eyeteeth to redo this place; what a plus for her resume. But if she'd gone into the oil business with her father, he wouldn't be so insistent she marry a man who could run it when he was gone.

She walked into the kitchen and found J.P. sitting at the table with coffee and a newspaper. What was his game? she wondered. Last night she'd been ready for his come-on. But he was barely civil when he'd removed the handcuffs. Then he'd made no protest when she'd gone upstairs right after dinner.

She'd expected him to suggest a walk in the garden. A visit to her room under the pretext of making sure she was comfortable. Something. But she hadn't seen him again. Was he trying to lull her into a false sense of security before he slithered in for the kill? There was an aura of intelligence about him, and she reminded herself to be on her toes. Until the sheriff arrived.

He would be there sometime this morning. J. P. Patterson didn't know her father's rent-a-thug had spilled his guts to her about everything. In just a little while, she would expose him for the snake he was in front of local law enforcement. The prospect made her decidedly cheerful.

"Good morning," she said.

He looked up. "Good morning."

"Where's your mother?"

"I'm not sure. If you're hungry, there's a buffet set up in the dining room."

"Why aren't you in there?"

"I prefer the kitchen."

So did she. And Jordan found she was hungry. She went into the room, which had a table long enough to land a 747 on, and picked up one of the two remaining plates on the sideboard. Then she lifted lids on the array of chafing dishes. She took some scrambled eggs, a Belgian waffle with strawberries and a dash of cream, a slice of ham and some fruit. There was a lovely silver carafe of coffee, and she settled a delicate china cup beneath the spigot then pushed back the handle to let it flow. It smelled wonderful.

When she sat down across from J.P. in the kitchen, he glanced at her plate. "I see yesterday's ordeal hasn't affected your appetite."

"Nothing like a kidnapping to stimulate a girl's palate," she said.

"I would expect someone who can't remember their own name to be more agitated."

If it wasn't Mr. Happy. She studied his narrow-eyed expression and thought about his distrustful tone. Was this the best he could do? If his goal was to make her dislike him, he was wildly successful.

"I sense a lack of trust. Are you suspicious by nature? Or merely projecting your own character onto others?"

"There's nothing wrong with my character. But I don't trust you," he admitted.

"Really?" This was good.

"Look, I'm going to be honest with you."

"Honesty is the best policy," she said virtuously. His eyes darkened a fraction, and she knew he'd caught her sarcasm.

"You noticed that I'm a wealthy man."

"Yeah. Like I said, the castle is a clue."

"Because of that, women throw themselves at me."

"You mean they're not attracted by your looks and sensitivity?" she asked sweetly.

"It started in high school and escalated from there."

He was probably telling the truth. She was an heiress; she knew all come-ons weren't sincere.

"Women do outrageous things to be noticed," he continued.

"So do men," she said pointedly.

"They do things like staking out the road to my home and pretending to be a victim," he finished, staring at her.

"Then why did you stop yesterday?" she asked, trying to trip him up.

"That's a good question. I've been asking myself the same thing."

"Did you come up with a good answer?"

He shrugged. "Probably the one in ten chance that you really did need help."

Jordan stared at him, searching for a chink in his facade. He was good, she thought. She almost believed him. At least her father had picked a man smart enough to keep the game interesting. If he'd come on to her in a smarmy way, she'd have shut him down faster than Miami in a hurricane. But clearly he was playing his part to the hilt. He was probably telling her this for sympathy, trying to bond so that they'd have something in common when her memory came back. He had no reason to know she was on to him and faking the amnesia.

"I really did need help," she said. "Thanks to you—"

Audrey walked into the kitchen and smiled. "Good morning, Jane."

"Mrs. Patterson."

"J.P., the sheriff arrived while I was out in the garden. I've shown him into the parlor. If you'll both join us there when you've finished eating?"

Jordan glanced at the half-eaten food on her plate,

then stood. "I've had enough, thanks. It's time to get this over with."

"I agree." J.P. came around the table and looked down at her.

Jordan would swear he was trying to intimidate her. It wouldn't work.

They walked through the house to a room near the front door. In the parlor stood a tall man about J.P.'s age and height wearing a beige shirt and matching trousers with olive-green and tan stripes down the leg. If the uniform hadn't been a clue, the badge on his chest said loud and clear that this good-looking man with light brown hair and green eyes was the sheriff.

When he saw them, a wide grin revealed very white teeth and laugh lines around his eyes. "Hey, J.P. It's been too long. We were supposed to have a beer together."

"Rick." J.P. grinned back and shook his hand. "It's good to see you. I've been busy with work."

"Me, too," the other man said. "We're going to have to put a date on the calendar."

"I'll have my secretary call you." J.P. looked at her. "Rick and I went through school together."

"How nice," Jordan said.

"From kindergarten through the twelfth grade," Audrey added.

Jordan smiled tightly. "It can't be a bad thing to have friends in the sheriff's department."

Rick looked at her. "I wasn't always in law enforcement. I managed to get into trouble a time or two. In high school, J.P. was voted most likely to take over the world. I was voted most likely to wind up in jail."

"And you did," Jordan commented. "In a manner of speaking."

Audrey gave the sheriff a hug. "How's your mother, Rick?"

"Doing fine, Mrs. P. I'll say hello to her for you."

"Let's all sit down," Audrey said. She took Jordan's hand and sat beside her on a green-and-gold brocade love seat. J.P. stood beside them.

The sheriff remained standing, backlit by the beveled-glass window. He looked at Jordan. "Sorry I couldn't get out here last night. The department was swamped. What's this about a kidnapping?"

J.P. should be the one answering that question. But her dream of humiliating him in front of the sheriff had gone down the tubes. They were boyhood buds, which explained how Audrey Patterson knew the sheriff had the sensitivity of a gnat. Under the circumstances, revealing J.P.'s part in this conspiracy would be a waste of time. Number one, she was on his turf and unlikely to get any support. Number two, his mother was obviously not in on the plan. Audrey Patterson was a sweetie. Jordan had no wish to hurt her by exposing her son in her presence.

"A lot of it is a blur." That part was true. Terror had a way of blurring the facts. "Then I remember riding in a car for what seemed like hours. I don't know how long it actually was. I was handcuffed to the passenger handle."

"Then what?"

"He parked on a road in the middle of nowhere. And we waited." That was true, too. "I told him I had to go to the bathroom."

The sheriff nodded his understanding. "Then what happened?"

"He unlocked the cuff, and I got out of the car."

"Can you remember what the perp looked like?"

"Early twenties. Brown hair."

"How tall?"

She tried to remember. "Not so tall that I couldn't give him a knee to the groin." Both men winced at that, but it was small satisfaction. "Shorter than both of you."

"Any tattoos? Distinguishing marks?"

She thought back and realized she really couldn't remember. "Not that I can recall."

The sheriff looked up from the notebook where he'd been jotting down her comments. "I did some checking, and there are no reports of a kidnapping and no one missing who fits your description."

No surprise there. It wasn't really a kidnapping, and she wasn't missing. J.P. had probably been in touch with her father to let him know the plan was working perfectly.

"What does that mean, Rick? In non-sheriff terms," Audrey added.

"It means I have very little to go on to learn her identity." He put his hat back on. "So, I'll take her back to town with me. Put her picture out there and see what we can come up with."

Jordan decided going with the sheriff would be best. She'd tell him her side of what happened and maybe he would help her find transportation back home. Somehow she would come up with a way to get through to her father that this stunt was an incredible invasion of her privacy.

"Thank you, Sheriff," she said. "I'd appreciate any help you can give me."

"Rick to the rescue," J.P. said.

The smile of satisfaction on his face really rubbed Jordan the wrong way. Along with the word *rescue*.

Her hero seemed relieved to be getting rid of her. She just didn't get it.

"I won't hear of it," Audrey said. "Jane, I think it would be best for you to stay here with us."

"Mother, we don't have the resources to help," J.P. pointed out. "Rick has computers and contacts within the law-enforcement community."

"And if he can't find her identity, what then?" Audrey asked. "Where will she go? Where will she stay? Who will take care of her?"

"Mrs. P., there are agencies to help out—city, county and state. She'll be well taken care of."

"Bureaucracy? I don't think so." Audrey shook her head. "She remembered more details today about what happened to her than she did yesterday. Obviously being here overnight helped. Rest and relaxation is working. It proves my theory that if she feels safe and secure her memory will come back."

"Mrs. Patterson," Jordan said, "It's very kind of you. I can't tell you how much I appreciate your concern. But it's probably best if I go with the sheriff. I've imposed on *you* too much," she said, then slid a glare in J.P.'s direction.

"Jane, dear," Audrey said, taking her hand. "It's no imposition. We enjoy having you here."

"Mother, she's a stranger. It's Rick's job to help strangers. Right, Sheriff?"

"J.P.'s right, ma'am," the sheriff said.

Audrey glared at her son. "J.P., I'm surprised at you. You, too, Rick Michaels. No man is an island. We need to reach out to each other."

"But she's not a man, and we don't know anything about her," J.P. pointed out.

"I know all I need to. And you're very well aware

that I'm an excellent judge of character. I absolutely won't hear of her leaving. And that's final.''

''It's not really up to you, Mom.'' He looked at Jordan. ''Are you going to drag this out?''

Drag it out? Her? Anger roared through Jordan and settled in her chest until she could hardly breathe. He'd started this. Him and her father. She'd been bullied and terrified. Ripped from her life and dumped in the middle of nowhere. And this bozo had the nerve to imply this was her fault? He acted like he wanted her gone. Then what would he do? Another kidnapping? Something worse? In cahoots with her father? The two of them had to be stopped.

Talking to her father about his previous stunts hadn't worked. Words weren't enough. She needed a statement—something big. Something the two of them would understand. But what? Her father obviously wanted her with J.P. Sooner or later he would make a move on her. This suspicious act was no doubt a psychological ploy to keep her off balance.

Well, she would turn the tables on him and her father. Take them both down in one fell swoop. For men like Harman Bishop and J. P. Patterson, failure to achieve a desired objective was not an option. If she let on that she knew what they were up to and went quietly, it was nothing more than a bump in the road. If she stayed and played them like a finely tuned fiddle, failure would be bigger and more humiliating. *That* would scuttle their plans and teach them not to mess with Jordan Bishop.

When J.P. came on to her, she would cut him off at the knees. She would teach him and her father not to meddle in her life.

"Jane, are you all right?" Audrey squeezed her hands. "What do you say?"

She'd planned to spend her vacation relaxing. Her spirit could relax better after a bit of retaliation. She felt safe. Her father knew J.P., probably through business. But no matter how angry she was with Harman Bishop, she didn't for a moment believe he would harm her or choose a man who would hurt her physically.

Although she felt guilty taking advantage of Audrey's generous nature, she needed time to plan. Jordan would find a way to make it up to her.

She met Audrey's gaze. "You're very kind. I gladly accept your hospitality."

Chapter Four

Sitting at his desk in the library, J.P. looked up from the spreadsheet on his computer screen. Jane was in the room. He couldn't even say a sound had alerted him to her presence. He wished she'd come in making as much noise as a high school marching band, but she hadn't. Somehow he'd just sensed she was there. And that was damned annoying. She stood just inside the door, staring with a sort of awestruck expression at the floor-to-ceiling bookcases ringing the perimeter of the room.

"May I help you?"

She whirled at the sound of his voice and pressed a palm to her chest. "Good heavens, you startled me. I didn't know anyone was in here."

Like hell she didn't. "I'm working."

"Surely you have an office?"

"You're in it," he said.

"I mean outside the home." One delicate, dark eyebrow arched. "Or are you hanging around the house to keep an eye on me?"

So she'd noticed. Unfortunately, he'd noticed she wasn't hard on the eyes. And the ridiculous outfit she wore did nothing to lessen the impact. His mother's sweats were too long and baggy for Jane and the snug T-shirt molded to her upper body. Both items only emphasized how small she was.

"I have an office. But I'm working from home today in order to spend some time with my mother. Where is she, by the way?"

"You mean did I whack her and dispose of the body in the rose garden?"

Sass, he thought intrigued. The quick comeback was evidence of a keen intellect. And whatever characteristics she might possess, shyness wasn't one of them. He tucked the information away.

"I see you have an imagination and you know how to use it," he commented.

"Maybe I'm a creative person." She stood in front of his desk and tapped a finger against her lips. "I've been giving it some thought. And I think maybe I do something with interior design and decoration."

"Really?" He leaned back in his tufted leather chair and studied her.

"I think I had one of those memory bursts your mother mentioned." Her gaze swung in a semicircle and touched on elements of the room. "Just looking around this house, ideas are coming to me—material swatches, paint chips, traffic patterns, rearranging furniture. I have a very strong sense that I do decorating for a living. So there may be some truth in what your mother says about a connection between R and R and memory recovery."

"I see."

"And by the way, I didn't whack her. She said when I saw you to tell you she forgot about a doctor's appointment. It's her yearly checkup and you shouldn't worry. And if her doctor is running as late as usual, she'll probably stay at a hotel in town."

Just like Audrey to take in a stray and leave everything to him. J.P. sighed. "Well, here we are then."

"Yes." She glanced at the bookshelves. "This room reminds me of the scene in *Beauty and the Beast* when Belle goes into the library for the first time."

"Another memory flash?" he asked.

"Apparently. Speaking of the beast," she said, her gaze narrowing on him. "Are you always so warm and inviting?"

"I'm trying to impress you."

"You could have fooled me." As she studied him, she folded her arms beneath her breasts.

He didn't miss the interesting things the movement did to her chest. After several moments he realized she was expecting him to say something. "What?"

"I'm very confused about something."

"Memory loss does that," he said dryly.

"It's not that. It's you. You're a reasonably good-looking man. But grumpy as a wounded bear."

"Are *you* always so warm and inviting?" he asked.

"I don't remember."

"Do you have a point?"

"Yes. I'm having trouble understanding why women throw themselves at you. I know you said it's about the money. But considering your personality, it can't be worth it. You seem unjustifiably suspicious."

"I have my reasons."

"Maybe it has something to do with 'Takes one to know one'?" she suggested.

"Are you implying that you're a cheat or that I'm less than honest?"

"Are you a businessman?" she asked, ignoring the reference to her.

She knew he was. A smart girl like her would have done her research. But he decided to play along to see where she was going with this. "Yes."

"It's a well-known fact that for a businessman the most important thing is the bottom line. More important even than integrity."

He met her gaze. "That's a very interesting observation for a woman who claims to have no memory."

She leaned against the corner of his desk. He couldn't help noticing the way the soft fleece pulled tight across her thigh and emphasized the curve of her hip. But that's exactly what a con-woman would do—distract him with whatever assets she possessed. And she distracted him better than most.

"Your mother said all memories are buried but still active in the subconscious."

"Is that so?" He folded his arms over his chest.

"Yes. Her theory is that bursts of awareness—like the interior decorator thing—will happen. Eventually all the memories will fit together and form a complete picture. Like a puzzle."

He nodded. "And we should take this as gospel because my mother is an expert on the subject?"

"What kind of son are you? It's not nice to make fun of your mother."

"I'm not making fun of her. But the advice she's dishing out comes from books and movies. It's fiction.'' Not unlike Jane's scheme to find a path into his life.

"It makes as much sense as anything else. Don't you ever wonder how researchers reach their conclusions when they do a study on babies or people in comas? These test subjects can't talk. The scientists are going strictly on observation. How reliable can the data be?''

Actually, he hadn't wondered about it. But she had a point. "Did you have a reason for wandering in here? Other than to bug me?''

"I didn't even know you were here,'' she retorted. "Don't look now, but your suspicions are showing again.''

"Were you looking for something to read?'' he said, choosing to ignore her editorializing.

"Your mother advised me to wander around and stimulate my senses.''

Jane was certainly stimulating his. Her beauty was a given, but her voice, with its hint of sandpaper, scraped along his nerve endings. Her fragrance drifted to him, filling his head with the scent of her skin, making him think of a field of wildflowers. Three out of five senses were stimulated, making his hands tingle at the thought of touching her softness. The longer she hung out here with him, the harder it would be to resist tasting the area where her neck curved into her shoulder.

She was becoming more difficult to ignore by the second. And all of that made him angry as a wounded bear, just as she'd said. He *knew* she was up to something. So his reaction made absolutely no sense. The fact that he was on to her should have protected him.

"And what does my mother think stimulating your

senses will do?'' he asked. He'd meant to sound cynical and sarcastic, but the hoarseness in his voice sort of defused the overall effect. He cleared his throat.

"She thought it might trigger some memories."

"Is she right?"

Jane glanced around. "I think so. I remembered being an interior decorator."

"Do you remember your name?"

"Not yet." Her gaze lifted to one of the bookcases behind him. "How do you get books down from up there?"

"You've obviously forgotten, but there's a handy little invention called a ladder." He pointed to the corner behind her where the sliding apparatus was parked until needed.

"Ah," she said, glancing over her shoulder. "Very cool. This room is completely amazing. I love to read."

His eyebrow went up. "Memory burst."

"Apparently. A person with amnesia could get shell-shocked from all the bursting memories." She looked at him and had the audacity to grin wickedly. "Do you mind if I wander around?"

He minded very much. "Help yourself."

Interesting, he thought. She wasn't glaring at him anymore. She was flirting. And he had to admit he didn't hate it. He didn't exactly like it. He didn't trust it, but it sure beat the heck out of glaring.

She strolled across the distressed wood floor and glanced at titles, pulling out a book here and there, then replacing them. After a few minutes, she slid the ladder to a spot across from his desk, directly in his line of vision. She was barefoot because she only had one high heel and his mother had no shoes that would fit. He noticed Jane's toes were painted red as she put one bare foot on the first rung and climbed up, stopping at every shelf to check out a book. When she reached the ladder's limits, she gazed up. Her attention was obviously captured by something and she reached above her head, stretching out a toned, tanned arm.

J.P.'s gaze slid to the sliver of skin on her midriff revealed by the stretch. The creamy flesh made him swallow hard. She pulled a book from the shelf and checked out the cover, then the back. After opening it and reading what he guessed was the first page, she climbed down the ladder, her hips swaying. Even the baggy sweatpants couldn't hide the motion and his mouth went dry.

On the floor again, she turned toward him. ''I'm sorry to have disturbed you.''

''You didn't,'' he lied.

''Good.'' Then she walked out of the room and shut the door after herself.

J.P. ran his fingers through his hair as he let out a long breath. Apparently he'd been whacked with the stupidity stick because clearly he was attracted to the beautiful liar. This wasn't the first time he'd been stupid. But this time his mother liked Jane. He hadn't contradicted Audrey's declaration that she was an exceptional judge of character because he'd found out the hard way that it was true. If he'd listened to her, he'd have saved himself a lot of heartache and humiliation.

But even with Audrey's approval, he had a hard time believing that ''Jane'' was an innocent victim. Annoyance tightened his gut. It bugged the hell out of him that she thought he was dumb enough to be fooled by her act or foolish enough to be blinded by her pretty face.

She would find out she was sadly mistaken on both counts.

About eight o'clock that night, Jordan closed the book she'd just finished reading and stood, stretching her stiff muscles. She hadn't seen J.P. since dinner. If he was interested in her, hiding out in his cave and ignoring her was a funny way to show it. He'd worked there all day, coming out only for meals. This evening he'd gone back to wait for a fax. If he wasn't lying. Clearly it was from someone like himself who worked like he had no life.

It figured that the man Harman Bishop had chosen for her was a clone of himself. All her life he'd ignored her and her mother in favor of his business. It was like his mistress. In fact, Jordan suspected that behavior had contributed to her mother's death. When Elizabeth Bishop had become ill, her husband had buried himself even deeper in work. And her mother just hadn't had the will to fight the cancer alone. After his own brush with death, her father had simply switched his obsession from business to marrying Jordan to a man who would run his business.

Apparently her father felt so strongly that J. P. Patterson was the right man, he'd arranged this elaborate scheme to nudge her into falling in love. So not happening, she thought. Even if she was interested, she'd promised herself she would never marry someone like her father who put work first. But she didn't have to marry J.P. to be curious.

She glanced around the great room, marveling again at the dichotomy of warmth and formality in the castle architecture. She was curious *and* bored because she'd been by herself all day. It was time to bring her book back to the library, she thought, moving down the hall.

She stopped in the doorway and glanced into the room where J.P. was staring at his computer screen. Was isolating himself and ignoring her all about reverse psychology? Had J.P. gone to her father for this strategy, to get pointers? And what possible pointers could her father contribute since he didn't know the first thing about her? How was J.P. going to win her hand if he wouldn't even talk to her? It didn't seem an especially aggressive strategy and if he was like her father, aggressive would be his middle name.

But this waiting was driving her nuts. Why hadn't he made his move? She wanted him to come on to her so she could shut him down and get this over with. Maybe she should go in his cave, invade his personal space and shake him up. Is that what he wanted? Make her come to him? Would that be playing into his hands? Even so, it wouldn't work because she knew his ultimate goal. She could protect herself. Revenge was the name of her game, and she wanted to make him squirm. If he was like her father, the best way to do that was to disrupt his work.

She walked into the library. "Hi."

He pulled his gaze from the computer screen. "Hi."

"What are you working on?" She sat in one of the tufted leather wing chairs in front of his desk and crossed one leg over the other.

"An oil company merger."

"I see." Her father was in oil. That must be how their paths had crossed.

His gaze settled on the monitor again. He stared at it with the single-minded focus of a man looking at a naked woman. She studied him. His work habits might be a carbon copy of her father's, but his looks put him in a class by himself. The dark, brooding expression on his face made her think of the beast she'd mentioned earlier. What would it be like to be the object of such intense scrutiny? Her stomach did a funny little jump at the thought.

There was a bit of curl in his almost black hair, around the temples and just above his collar. Did he need a haircut? Was his hair usually shorter to keep the curl under control? Darned if her fingers didn't tingle at the thought of sliding through the dark strands. He glanced at her and his blue eyes smoldered, with what she wasn't sure.

"Is there something you wanted?" he asked.

"Yes." She had nothing to lose by being direct. "I want to know if you're avoiding me."

"Trying to." He glanced back at the computer.

Apparently being direct was contagious. His slightly abrasive response surprised her since she'd expected him to get smarmy. Annoying man, she thought. His attitude made her more determined to be the burr under his saddle.

"Have you ever heard the expression 'All work and no play makes J.P. a dull boy'?"

"No."

"Did your fax come in?"

"Not yet."

She continued staring at him. She could out-stubborn a mule. "Do you think it's going to?"

"I couldn't say."

"Because that would mean someone else is putting in work hours like you."

"And your point?" he said, meeting her gaze.

"It's nuts to work hours like this."

"And how do you know this?"

"I'm not sure," she said. "Just a vague impression plus innate common sense. It doesn't take memories to know that working this long and hard can't be good for you."

"And why would you care about me?"

"I wasn't saying that I do. Just that you're nuts."

His gaze narrowed on her. "Are you always this irritating?"

"No." That was pretty close to the truth. Normally, she bent over backward to avoid being a pain. After all, she worked in a business that depended on customer service. But in his case, she was willing to make an exception. "At least I don't think so."

"Look, Jane, I have work to do."

"Can I help?"

"No."

They stared at each other some more. She was waiting for him to get the message that she wasn't leaving. "Are you sure there's nothing I can do to help you?"

"Don't you have a book to read?" he asked, frowning.

"I finished it."

"Fast reader."

"I guess so." She continued to look at him when he returned his gaze to the screen. Shifting in the chair, she recrossed her legs and let out a long breath.

"What about television?" he asked, not looking at her.

"What about it?"

"There must be something on that you'd like to watch."

"I don't remember what I like to watch."

That was actually true. She'd been working long hours herself, which was how she knew the time he was putting in was nuts. It took a lot of blood, sweat and tears to get an office open and that's what she'd been doing. After college, she'd joined Elite Interiors, a large interior design firm. They were expanding and had put her in charge of getting the branch office open in Dallas, about an hour from Sweet Spring and her friends. It was finally up and running smoothly, which was why she'd decided to take her first vacation in two years.

"You could turn it on and just channel surf," he suggested. "Something might catch your eye."

"I don't think that's what your mother had in mind."

"What are you talking about?"

"Before she left, she mentioned that she was glad you were working from home today because I shouldn't be alone."

His gaze met hers and there was that sizzle that seemed to burn her skin. "Did she really?"

"Yes. Her comment implied you have an office somewhere else but were choosing to work here instead. When I stumbled in earlier, it was because I had no idea where your home office was. It's a pretty big castle."

"I see."

His tone said he didn't see at all. And she couldn't care less.

"Audrey said it could be traumatic if my memory returns all at once." She tried to look pathetic which was tough since bugging him was the most fun she'd had all day. "In case that happened, she was glad I had company. But that all depends on your definition of company.''

"What's yours?''

"Certainly not wandering around a reconstituted castle with only a book to talk to.''

"It's not reconstituted. That implies pouring water on it.''

"You know what I meant,'' she said.

He leaned back in his chair and settled his linked hands over his flat-as-a-washboard abdomen. ''I'm getting the feeling that you don't plan to leave me alone.''

"Really? Why?''

"Because you're still here.''

"Yes.'' And now that she had him where she wanted him, what was she going to do with him? Did she let him direct the action? Or should she take control? Definitely the latter. ''Want to play a game?''

"I thought that's what we were doing.''

Did he feel it, too? Was he starting to crack? ''Actually, I meant a board game.'' She thought a moment, then added, ''Or we could take a walk, and you could show me the garden in the moonlight.''

He looked as if he would rather suck a jalapeno dipped in lemon. ''If you're not going to leave me alone, I choose a board game.''

Again she had to question his strategy. The offer of a walk in the moonlight was a golden opportunity she'd put on a silver platter worthy of the folks who used to live in this castle. And he'd chosen the alternative. Had he changed his mind about the deal with her father after meeting her? That pricked her pride a bit. She didn't consider herself a raving beauty, but she wouldn't have to wear a bag over her head in public either.

"How about Trivial Pursuit?" she suggested. It symbolized his intentions perfectly.

One of his eyebrows lifted. "Seems an odd choice."

"Because I can't remember who I am?"

"Yes," he answered, in a tone that clearly said, "Duh."

"Are you aware that people afflicted with Alzheimer's disease are encouraged to stimulate their minds with crossword puzzles and word games?"

"And how do you know that?"

"I just do," she snapped.

His snarky, suspicious comments were starting to get under her skin. She admitted she was being less than honest with him, but ultimately right was on her side. He'd done a bad thing first.

J.P. stared at her. "Playing a game where the winning outcome is determined by the players' comprehensive knowledge of trivia seems like taking advantage of someone with amnesia. It feels like piling on."

His voice lowered in a sort of sensual way on the last words. She got an instant visual of bodies pressed together in a horizontal position, and it sent a little shiver dancing over her skin. That wasn't supposed to happen and it tweaked her temper.

"If you don't want to play, just say so."

Jordan stood, fully expecting that he would dismiss her and keep working. It's what her father would do. She wanted to get this charade over with, but apparently he had his own timetable. She could lead the snake to his target, but she couldn't make him strike.

"The board games are stacked in the closet in the great room," he said.

Well, would wonders never cease. He'd accepted her challenge; it was put up or shut up.

"Okay."

She walked out of the room and found the closet he meant. Flipping on the light switch just outside the door, she walked through the opening and saw a neatly stacked selection of games. There were several editions of Trivial Pursuit, and she chose the Twentieth Anniversary version. After shutting off the light and closing the door, she went back to the library. She decided that she could explain answers she got right under the umbrella that only the specific details of her life were a blur.

She looked at the scattered paperwork on his desk and decided to set the game up somewhere else. In the corner there was a coffee table between two love seats covered in a beige-colored chenille with a floral pattern embedded in the material. It was subdued but elegant and the very latest thing.

She set the box on the table and opened it, then unfolded the board and pulled out the game pieces. J.P. sat on the sofa across from her and picked up the single die.

"Roll it and we'll see who goes first," she said.

He did and got a six. She got a two.

He met her gaze. "Score one for me."

Enjoy it, she thought, because you're not going to score with me.

He rolled again and from the center he chose to move to a space for a News question. She pulled a card from the dispenser on the table between them. "What Long Islander got in hot water with Albion prison authorities for dying her hair with purple Kool-Aid?'' she asked, then turned it over to read the answer.

He narrowed his gaze on her. ''That's not news.''

''Yes, it is. It's on the card.''

''News is a dip in the stock market. It's an earthquake in China. Or India invading Pakistan.''

''You don't get to decide what is or what isn't an acceptable question. If you don't know the answer, simply say so. But don't make it the game's fault.''

''Okay.'' He leaned forward and rested his elbows on his knees as he met her gaze. ''I have no idea who would be dumb enough to dye her hair with Kool-Aid in prison.''

''Amy Fisher,'' she said triumphantly. ''My turn.''

She rolled the die and moved to a pink square for a Sound and Screen question. He slid a card from the dispenser and looked at it, frowning as he read silently.

''Are you going to let me in on it any time soon?'' she asked.

He shook his head then read, ''What gooey substance do audience members dribble over naked Karen Finley during her performance-art piece *Shut Up and Love Me?*''

She stared at him, the way his eyes seemed to burn like blue flames. Her skin grew warm, and she didn't think it was from embarrassment because he'd said the word naked.

She cleared her throat. ''I have never heard of Karen Finley or her performance art. But I'm going to make an educated guess that the dribbling substance would have to be paint.''

The corners of his mouth curved up. ''Your guess is not educated enough. The answer is honey.''

"That would have been my second guess."

For the next two hours they played the game, a pleasant diversion from the one they'd been playing since she met him. Amazingly enough, she had a good time. J.P. actually had a sharp intelligence and a keen sense of humor. She learned his vulnerable categories and he discovered hers. They were neck and neck, both of their game wheels filled with colored plastic pies. They'd each gone in and out of the center and missed questions that would have won the game.

Finally, J.P. rolled and wound up back in the center with the game on the line. She picked a new card. Without looking at the question, she decided to ask him a pink one. Entertainment trivia was way off his radar. For a workaholic, business *was* his entertainment. All work and no play made J.P.—neither dull, nor unattractive now that she thought about it.

"What TV-trash host inspired a London opera that boasts the aria *Do You Ever Wonder Why Your Imaginary Friend Committed Suicide?*"

He ran his fingers through his hair. "Do you ever wonder who comes up with this stuff?"

"Someone with no life. But you're stalling," she accused.

"I don't think there's a time limit on reasoning this out, is there?"

"We agreed on two minutes. If you can't figure it out by then, it's not happening."

"Okay." He blew out a long breath. "The clue is trash-TV host." He thought for a minute. "What's the name of that guy everyone makes fun of? Where the people on the show wind up clocking each other with chairs?"

"Why should I help you?" she asked.

"Because I cut you some slack on that sports question that got you a pie."

"You didn't do me any favors," she defended.

One of his eyebrows went up. "The golfer with the animal first name is technically not the correct answer."

"I got his name—eventually. Besides, Tiger Woods is the only golfer I know. But this is for the entire game and bragging rights. You have to do it without help. *Both* names."

"Okay. TV-trash host." He thought for several moments, then a gleam stole into his eyes. "I can see him. Glasses. Blond or silver hair. Jerry Springer."

"Darn it," she said, tossing the card into the middle of the board. Then she pointed at him. "Don't you dare gloat."

"What happened to bragging rights?"

"That's different from gloating," she said. "And if you know what's good for you, you'll refrain from that behavior."

"Or what?" he asked, grinning with satisfaction.

"I'll superglue your computer paper together."

He laughed. "In that case, humility is my middle name."

She stood and lifted her arms, then leaned back and turned from side to side to stretch her cramped muscles. When she looked at him, his expression went from humorous to hard as granite and the muscle in his lean jaw jumped.

He glanced at his wristwatch. "It's getting late. Obviously that fax isn't coming. I'm going to turn in."

"Good night."

"Yeah." He turned away and walked out of the room without giving her a look.

In a sort of shocked surprise, Jordan sat down and put the game pieces away. What had just happened? she wondered. They were communicating. He even laughed and smiled. She'd been so sure he was going to do *something* about getting more personal. Then he'd walked out as if he couldn't leave her fast enough.

What the heck was he doing? Nothing, was her answer. She looked down at the borrowed clothes she was wearing. Maybe if she got naked and poured honey over herself.

No, that would be playing into his hands. Surely he was trying to lull her into a false sense of something. Show some interest, then retreat. Make her yearn for contact with another human, with a man. No, she didn't yearn for anything from him except satisfaction.

When he moved on her, she would tell him exactly what she thought of him. Then he would turn on Harman Bishop. If they had any sort of business association it probably wouldn't survive what she had planned. That should make her point with her father. And he would finally leave her alone.

She would get her life back.

Chapter Five

The following day, J.P. sat in front of his computer and wearily rubbed his hands over his face. He'd had a rough night. It wasn't the worst he'd ever slept, but probably ranked in the top five. The memory of Jane, arms stretched over her head, shirt sliding up to reveal the soft, pale skin of her abdomen—a sight that made his palms itch to touch her—was burned into his brain. How could he rest with his motor revved up all night? He wouldn't have slept at all if he'd given in to his urge to pull her into his arms. Better to retreat and look like an idiot than kiss her and prove it.

And he was doing it again now—retreating. Hiding in his office. Hoping Jane wouldn't invade his sanctuary again. It was almost noon and so far she'd left him alone.

"J.P.?" Audrey peeked into the room.

"Mother." He stood, relief coursing through him. Reinforcements had finally arrived. He rounded his desk.

She walked over and kissed his cheek. "Hello, dear."

"How was your checkup?"

"Fine. Test results will be back next week, but the doctor says I have the body of a woman twenty years younger."

"Good."

"Where's Jane?"

"I haven't seen her this morning."

"It's almost midday, dear."

"So it is."

She put her hands on her hips. "She's our guest. Have you been ignoring her the whole time I was gone?"

"Of course not." He'd tried but Jane had a way of invading his space and his senses, making it impossible to overlook her. "We played a game last night."

"Do I want to know what kind of game?" she asked, arching her eyebrow suggestively.

"Trivial Pursuit."

Audrey Patterson was a hopeless romantic. J.P. had tried to protect his mother from the fact that being wealthy had taken the romance out of his life. His money was the only thing that stirred up chemistry for some women. There was probably someone sincere out there, but he wasn't interested in wading through the wanna-bes to find her.

He didn't make a habit of introducing Audrey to the women he saw socially. She wanted him to settle down and fall in love. Unfortunately, trusting a woman was a prerequisite for that and it just wasn't going to happen. But he didn't see any reason to come right out and tell her so.

"You and Jane played Trivial Pursuit?"

He nodded. "She said it would stimulate her mind."

"And did it stimulate anything?"

Me, he thought. "Not that I know of."

Audrey waited, then frowned when he didn't say more. "Come look at what I got for Val," she said.

"What have you bought now that's going to spoil my niece rotten?"

She slipped her hand into the crook of his elbow as they walked into the great room. Packages and bags were strewn on the floor and scattered across the sofa and chairs.

Audrey glanced at everything, pleasure glowing in her eyes. "It isn't spoiling my only granddaughter when these are gifts for her birthday. Can you believe she's going to be four?"

He shook his head. "Seems like she was just born."

He envied his sister. Cathy had fallen in love when she was in college and married after Kevin completed law school and passed the bar exam. He was on the legal team at Patterson, Inc. and was one of their best attorneys. Somehow Cathy's experiences hadn't included men wanting her just for her money. In the romance department she'd gotten all the Patterson luck.

"I hope you got her slot cars. Or a dump truck. Or maybe a fire engine. Or one of those fire hats with the lights and siren on it."

His mother looked at him sympathetically. "If you want boy toys, you need to do your manly duty to populate this family with children of the male persuasion."

"I don't want to rush it, Mom."

"For goodness' sake, you're over thirty. I don't think that's rushing into marriage."

"Actually, I was talking about rushing a relationship."

She sighed. "There's no such thing as rushing. Either it's right or it isn't. Instinct will tell you if a woman is the one for you. And you need to pay attention to those instincts because if you're waiting for a sign from heaven or lightning to strike, it's not going to happen."

"Mother, let it go—"

"J.P., one or two bad experiences shouldn't sour you on love and marriage."

"You should know better than anyone why I'm cautious."

"I take no satisfaction in being right about that underhanded hussy. I also think you need to get back on the horse."

"I will. Someday," he added.

Audrey slid him a resigned look before rustling through the bags and pulling out several boxes. "Valerie loves Polly Pocket. Look at this darling little set with the beauty parlor and nail salon. And this one with the tiny Jeep and surfboard. Isn't it adorable?"

He studied the package. "It's for girls, Mom."

"Poor J.P.," she said. "You're surrounded by women."

"There are worse things," he said.

"Like not being surrounded at all. It hurts my heart to see you this way, J.P."

"What way is that?"

"Alone," she said.

"So are you," he pointed out.

"True. But I had many years with a wonderful man

and two fantastic children to show for it. And I'll admit I'm lonely. At first it was all about missing your father. Now it's just being by myself.''

"Mom, you should have said something. I—"

"Stop right there," she said, holding up her hand. "I didn't mention it because I need anything from you. It's simply a statement of fact that I have a certain understanding of how you feel."

That's where she was wrong. "I'm very content."

Unless you counted last night. In which case he was lying like a rug.

His mother looked at him and sighed. "You're absolutely hopeless."

"Thank you."

Jane appeared in the doorway. "Audrey. You're back."

"Hello, dear." She moved to hug their guest. "Are you all right?"

"Fine."

"Where have you been?"

"Upstairs in the window-seat room. I was going to take a walk. The gardens and grounds here are so wonderful."

"Yes, I enjoy walking in them, too." Audrey studied her. "Any memory bursts?"

"Yes, actually. I remembered that I'm an interior designer."

His mother smiled her pleasure. "That's wonderful, dear. Obviously my strategy is working."

Jane looked at him. "I just wish it would work faster."

"You can't rush it, dear. Things will happen in their own good time. If you'd like, we can hire a private investigator to see what he can turn up."

"That's a good idea." Jane glanced at him, then said to his mother, "Did your checkup go well?"

Audrey nodded. "Fit as a fiddle."

"I'm glad to hear it." Jane moved into the room and stared at all the packages. "Apparently the clean bill of health sent you on the mother of all shopping sprees."

"Actually, it was more like necessity. My granddaughter, Val, is having a birthday soon."

"She's one lucky little girl."

"Spoiled rotten," J.P. said.

"It's a grandmother's prerogative to buy a lot of things. Besides, this isn't all for Valerie."

"Good," Jane said. "I hope you got something fun for yourself after being a good girl at the doctor."

"Actually, no. But I did get some things for you, dear," she said.

Jane pressed a palm to her chest. "Me? But you shouldn't have."

J.P. watched her closely, studying her reaction to his mother's announcement. Jane seemed genuinely surprised although he had trouble believing there was anything genuine about her.

Audrey waved away her protest. "Yes, I should have. You can't continue to wear my castoffs."

"They're fine."

"They'll need washing. We can't have you going naked."

She could be performance art, J.P. thought. Was there any honey handy?

"Seriously, Mrs. Patterson, I can't accept anything from you."

"Why not?"

"Because I—"

"It's not a big deal," Audrey said. "Just a pair of shorts and a top. Some jeans and a T-shirt. Some under things. I guessed at your size, but I thought anything is better than my old things that are too big for you. You're so tiny."

Jane definitely was that, he thought. She made a man feel manly, protective. How many men had fallen into her trap, making them want to take care of her?

"But, Mrs. Patterson, you don't know anything about me. What if I can't pay you back?"

"You're an interior decorator. You have a job."

"But what if I'm not a very good one? What if I don't get any clients? I may have no money to reimburse you."

J.P. recalled that the clothes she was wearing when he found her were of good quality. He suspected they weren't cheap. But the upscale outfit could have been nothing more than an investment in the scam. Something to throw him off by convincing him that she didn't need his money. Was this show of reluctance to accept anything simply designed to ingratiate herself? Then he looked at the expression on his mother's face. It had given her pleasure to shop for Jane. She would be disappointed if her kindness was refused.

"If you'd feel better," he said, "we could start a tab."

"Really, J.P., this isn't a bar." Audrey thought for a moment, then said, "We'll just keep track of what we spend. When Jane's memory returns, she can pay us back for any expenditures we've made on her behalf."

"I'd rather not take anything," Jane said. "What if I don't have any money? What if I'm already up to my eyeballs in debt? I think it would be foolish to take on more.''

''Nonsense,'' Audrey said.

J.P. couldn't agree more that this was nonsense. ''Mother's right. We can't have you going around naked while your clothes are in the wash.''

''Maybe I could do something to work for them now,'' she suggested.

Audrey put up her hand for silence. ''Dear girl,'' she said. ''I feel like an Amazon when I look at you wearing my clothes. They are practically falling off your tiny little body. It would please me if you would wear the new things. If we learn you're penniless, we'll simply let you work off the debt somehow. Would that satisfy your conscience?''

''When you put it like that? Yes.'' Jane smiled.

Audrey pulled a shoe box out of a bag. ''Here. It's just sneakers.''

Jane took the box and checked it out. ''How did you know my size?''

''I looked at your shoe.''

Jane pulled out the pristine white canvas shoes and smiled as if they were diamonds. ''Thank you.''

''You're quite welcome, dear. And please, don't worry about the money. The most important thing is R and R.''

''Rest and relaxation?'' Jane clarified.

''Almost,'' Audrey said. ''Relax and remember.'' She looked at the two of them. ''Have you had lunch?''

''I haven't,'' Jane said. ''I can't speak for J.P.''

''No,'' he said.

''Then let's see if there's anything in the kitchen.''

"You know the housekeeper stocks it weekly," J.P. reminded her.

"So she does." She looked at Jane. "Run upstairs and try on your new things and I'll fix something."

"Okay." Jane moved to the doorway, then turned back and smiled. "I'll hurry so I can give you a hand."

"Thank you, dear."

J.P. felt the power of her smile clear to his gut. Same as last night. She'd smiled a lot, and laughed. Him, too. He'd had fun. Wouldn't you know it was the first time in longer than he could remember that he'd had such a good time with any woman. And since his sister had used up all the good karma, his luck was to be attracted to a woman who was lying through her beautiful, pearly white teeth. There was no other logical explanation for her being abandoned practically on his doorstep with a preposterous story about being kidnapped. It was almost as good as the lie that led to his disastrous engagement. Was it his tragic flaw to be attracted to duplicitous women?

Audrey watched Jane leave, then said, "She's such a lovely girl. I hope she remembers who she is and who kidnapped her. Then the bastard can be put away and she'll be safe."

"Hmm," was all J.P. said.

This was bad. Audrey was already getting attached. How was he going to stop it? If he told her what he thought, she'd pooh-pooh it and say he was too suspicious. If he was going to convince her, he had to get Jane to tip her hand. She'd given him a funny look when she said she wished her memory would return faster. Her wariness was showing again. If he kept snarling at her, she would always be on guard.

It was time to change his strategy. He needed to make her think he'd accepted her story. Warm and inviting, that was the ticket. Look out, Ms. Doe. Nobody could do charming like J. P. Patterson.

The following morning, wearing her new jeans and T-shirt, Jordan went downstairs. It was heaven having clothes that fit. Even the tennis shoes. Audrey Patterson had a keen eye. Which made her wonder how Audrey had accepted Jordan so easily. And that thought led to the tiniest smidgeon of guilt. Actually more than a smidgeon—until she reminded herself what J.P. had done. She would have to worry about his mother later. One mission at a time.

She walked into the kitchen and the son in question was sitting at the table reading the newspaper. J.P. looked up when her shoes squeaked on the tile floor.

"Good morning," he said. "Did you sleep well?"

"Yes. Thank you."

"Can I get you a cup of coffee?"

"Don't get up. I'll get it." She walked over to the coffeemaker on the counter. Pointing to the mug sitting there she said, "Is this for your mother?"

"No. She's visiting my sister today. Making plans for my niece's birthday party. I left it there for you."

Hmm. "Thanks."

She took her full cup over to the table and looked at him. "Anything interesting in the paper?"

"The usual." His gaze slid over her, leaving heat in its wake. "The clothes fit good."

"Yes." As good as the shorts and top she'd worn yesterday when he kept watching her.

"Do you have any plans for the day?"

Was this a trick question? She was on vacation. He

probably knew that because her father did. She'd
planned to visit museums and art galleries. She'd figured on day trips to places she'd always meant to visit
but had missed because she was always too busy.
When she'd done all that, she'd decided to see movies
and rent the ones she'd intended to take in but couldn't
work into her schedule. Yes, she had plans. And he'd
ruined them. Now she had a mission that would safeguard any future plans.

She met his gaze. "Plans? Under the circumstances,
I don't have anything on my schedule."

"How do you feel about going out with me for the
day?"

"Now you're starting to scare me."

He grinned. And it wasn't the reluctant kind she'd
coaxed from him up until now. This was a full-on,
knock-a-girl-on-her-butt kind of smile. A take-no-
prisoners look, intended to dazzle, raise female pulses
and weaken knees.

"Don't be scared," he said.

She sat down across from him. "Who are you?
What have you done with J. P. Patterson?"

"I'm not different."

"On the contrary. I didn't recognize you without
the scowl."

"You're exaggerating," he said.

"I don't think so. You've done a complete about-
face. What's up with that? If your mother was here,
I'd figure you were trying to get me away from her.
But she's already gone. Any second I expect to hear
a rousing rendition of the *Twilight Zone* theme."

"Oh, come on."

"Seriously." She met his gaze and waited.

"All right. Here's the deal."

"I'm all ears."

He folded the paper and set it aside. "You got through to me. I'm turning over a new leaf. Just call me Mr. Congeniality."

"Oh, puhleeze." She took a sip of her coffee. "Are you avoiding work?"

Highly unlikely. Her father's clone would never commit that unpardonable sin. But she wanted to see his reaction.

"Actually, I've been working too hard. I've been putting in a lot of hours on this merger, and it's time for a break."

"Right."

"I thought maybe you'd like to take a drive to the local mall. You could probably use a few more things. And we could wander around, let your senses be overloaded with stimuli. Might trigger some memories." He shrugged.

He was certainly looking all innocent, and sexy. Dark hair neatly combed. Dressed in his yellow collared shirt with a tab front and his khaki trousers. He looked completely yummy. But what was he up to? She couldn't believe he was actually concerned about her. At best it was an act. At worst, part of the plot.

She wasn't falling for it. On the other hand, this change of personality might be a sign that he was getting ready to move in on her. And it was about darn time. The sooner she showed him up for the underhanded creep he was, the sooner she could get on with her vacation.

"What do you say, Jane? How can any woman resist a trip to the mall?"

"I say let's do it."

* * *

With J.P. by her side, Jordan strolled the main promenade of the mall past jewelry carts, cell phone booths and the kiosk with handmade leather purses. He had graciously offered to carry her bags with the few purchases she'd made. She didn't feel quite as guilty letting him pay for a bit of make-up, some nightclothes, and a couple outfits. It was the least he could do.

J.P. looked down at her. "I haven't seen a bright flash of light. Any memories bursting yet?"

"Nothing specific. But I would be willing to bet I like shopping."

"Yeah." He looked around. "This is a rhetorical question since I don't expect you to remember the answer. But is the mall always so busy?"

Someone jostled her, pushing her into him. She felt the heat and almost heard the sizzle when their arms brushed, skin on skin. It had happened before and she'd hoped her reaction would diminish. No such luck, so she put several inches between them, fast.

"It does seem like there are a lot of people."

"People is right," he said. "All kinds. Look at that girl with her hair in mohawk spikes." He stared. "The spikes are dyed red."

"So they are."

"I wonder how she gets it to stay like that. Is it superglue or a miracle hair product?"

Jordan glanced up at him, smiling at his quizzical expression. "How narrow-minded of you to make fun. She's just expressing herself."

He met her gaze. "You wouldn't be so tolerant if she put your eye out with one of those things. And the body piercing? She looks like she fell face first into a tackle box.''

She laughed. ''That's such an appropriate description.''

Under different circumstances, she would be having fun. Hanging out with a good-looking guy who had an above average sense of humor and carried her packages. He must meet a lot of women. Was all that stuff about them only wanting him for his money true?

''I can't help wondering about something.''

''What's that?'' he asked, glancing into a men's shoe store display window.

''It occurs to me that no one here knows you from a rock. You're just a guy walking the mall with a friend. No one knows you have money or live in a castle.''

He looked down at her. ''And your point would be?''

''You said women throw themselves at you because of your money. Surely you've met women who don't know anything about you and are attracted. I can't help wondering if you've ever had a relationship where money wasn't an issue.''

''I have. And how do you know none of them worked out?''

''You're not married.''

''Okay. That's true.'' He hooked his index finger through the handles of a plastic bag and slung it over his shoulder.

''Does the question of money always come up?''

''No, actually. I dated in high school and had a long-term relationship in college.''

''What happened?''

''In high school we were too young and drifted

apart. College—'' He shrugged. ''She was ready to get married, and I wasn't.''

''So you weren't in love with her,'' Jordan commented.

''What's love got to do with it? I think there's more to settling down than just that.''

''Be still my heart,'' she said wryly.

''I've always thought there was something to the idea of a guy sowing his wild oats. Then when he's ready to have children, he finds a compatible woman.''

''Again I say, be still my heart.'' She grinned at his exasperated expression. ''So aren't you ready to have children?''

''Actually, I've thought about it lately.''

''Then it must be the dreaded *dinero* problem rearing its ugly head?''

''I was ready to get married once. I thought I'd found the right woman.''

''What happened?'' Jordan asked. Glancing sideways at him, she could see the muscle in his jaw clench and his mouth compress into a straight line. If this was acting, he was doing a darn good job.

''Turned out I was wrong about her. Money was the main attraction.'' He met her gaze and let out a long breath. Tension drained from his expression. ''Now I'm gun-shy. Finding someone is difficult enough. Then you factor in the dreaded *dinero* issue and the window of possibilities closes just a little more.''

''So money adds another deal-breaking dynamic to an already difficult scenario and you refuse to participate?''

''Do you blame me?'' He slid her a wry look. ''Since that last fiasco, I haven't been especially eager to throw my hat in the matrimonial ring.''

She narrowed her gaze on him. Is that why he'd gone along with her father's scheme? Because women wanted his money and he knew she didn't need it? But why go to all the trouble? Why not just meet her and confess about his past? That seemed the best way to get the sympathy vote. Why did he think he needed to pretend to be her hero to trick her into falling in love with him?

The automatic exit doors whispered open, and they walked outside into the humidity. Crossing the street into the covered parking structure, she wondered about him. It was on the tip of her tongue to ask for details about his last romantic fiasco. How could he be sure the woman was only after his money? But that could be playing into his hands. A guy who would go along with this elaborate kidnapping scheme couldn't be trusted to tell the truth.

"Turnabout is fair play," he said. "I'd like to hear about your relationships—the good, bad and ugly."

As if she needed one, here was a reminder to keep on her toes. "And I'd like to tell you. Because that would mean I could remember who I am."

"I envy you," he said.

"Me?" she asked, surprised. "Why?"

He stopped beside his car and hit the keyless entry button. "It would be easier to have amnesia. No memories—good or bad."

"It's disconcerting," she said cautiously.

"It's damned annoying." One corner of his mouth tilted up, then he opened the vehicle's rear hatch and stowed her purchases. He closed it and looked down at her.

"Why annoying?" she asked.

"I spill my guts and without reciprocation because

you can't remember a love life. One-sided soul-baring is not fair and equitable.''

"Sorry," she said with a shrug. "If I could I would."

He opened the passenger door for her and waited as she climbed into the car and settled in the seat. Standing there looking at her, his eyes darkened. Tension suffused his features again, but Jordan knew it wasn't about his past. It was all about his present.

"If you made some new memories, you'd have something to share," he said.

Here it comes, she thought. Finally, he was going to make a pass at her. It was about time. She could tell him to take a long walk off a short pier—preferably wearing cement overshoes.

She met his gaze. "I certainly can't argue with that logic."

"If only love were logical," he said. Then he shut the door.

She blinked at the space where he'd been standing. Why didn't he kiss her? She'd been so sure he would. Some rebellious female part of her was seriously upset because the yearning to know what it would feel like to kiss him was strong. And getting stronger, darn it.

Because he'd been incredibly pleasant and fun to be around. But, she reminded herself, he wasn't pleasant. He was like her father who could be incredibly charming, too, when he wanted something. She couldn't afford to forget even for a moment what J.P. was up to.

He opened the driver's door and slid inside. "What would you say to a stop for ice cream?"

Ice cream? Not a drink? Clearly he was diabolical. The way he was taking his time and tweaking his tactics must be part of his plan to win her over. That made her all the more determined to frustrate his intentions. When he tried to kiss her or take this scenario up a notch, she would show him the same moves she'd used on that moron kidnapper. Then let Harman Bishop try to repair his professional relationship with J. P. Patterson.

Mixing business with pleasure wasn't a good idea. Twin workaholics should know that better than anyone. But they'd made this personal—and not in a good way. J.P. was shrewd and crafty. A game player if she'd ever met one.

He was good. But she would be better.

Chapter Six

"I'm so glad you're here to help me decorate for this birthday party, Jane. Cathy is eight months pregnant with baby number two, and J.P. is hopeless. When it comes to decorating I mean." Audrey tied a knot in the balloon she'd just blown up.

J.P. held tight to the end of his balloon so the air he'd given up for the cause wouldn't leak out. "I'm not hopeless."

"Challenged?" Jane offered.

"That's less harsh," he agreed.

The three of them were in the great room decorating for the party. His sister had twisted his arm to have it there not just because she was pregnant. She'd said none of Val's little friends had had their parties at a castle. Cathy freely admitted, without shame, that she was trying to outdo all the other parents. He liked his sister's in-your-face honesty. It was more than he could say for some people, he thought, looking at Jane.

J.P. couldn't believe a week had passed since he'd

found her by the side of the road. He was afraid his warm and inviting strategy was backfiring. Ever since his attitude adjustment and their trip to the mall, the line between being charming and being charmed was beginning to blur.

He hated shopping, but he'd had a good time with her. His world had gone mad. Sometimes he forgot for brief moments why he wanted to get rid of her and the idea of her gone was slowly losing its appeal.

Audrey looked at Jane. "Have you had any more memory bursts, dear?"

Jane shook her head. "Only flashes. But it's like I can't connect the dots."

"I've been thinking again about hiring a private investigator," Audrey said.

That got his attention. He tied a knot in his pink balloon and tossed it on the growing pile in the center of the room. "I didn't think you wanted to do that, Mom."

"I love having Jane here," Audrey said. "But it seems selfish not to do everything possible to help her find out who she is."

J.P. wondered how Jane would react to that suggestion. She had a banner spread out on the coffee table that said Happy Birthday, Valerie. She'd insisted on personalizing it and was working on filling in the letters. As she glanced up, her shiny, dark hair swung away from her face. Big brown eyes—beautiful eyes—gave nothing away. So much for the window to the soul thing.

"What do you think, Jane?" he asked.

"I think Audrey's right. You've both been very gracious, but it would be best for everyone if I got my life back. My only objection is the cost. It's only right that I reimburse you for everything, but I don't imagine investigators come cheap." She stared at him as if she was looking for his reaction. "What do *you* think?"

That was a good question. He rubbed the back of his neck. Since he was attempting to get her to lower her guard and slip up, he figured the correct response would be that he didn't mind if she stayed indefinitely.

"I think," he said, "that we should hold off on a private investigator for a bit."

"I'm not sure I agree, dear," Audrey countered. "Returning Jane to familiar surroundings might shock her into remembering."

"Maybe. But she's comfortable here. Right, Jane?"

"Yes. You've both been extremely hospitable. And me a total stranger."

J.P. studied her and wondered about her emphasis on the last word. "Then let's hold off just a little longer on a detective. Give her a chance to remember on her own."

"You're very kind," she said to him.

Kind? Why did the bland word bug him? It's not like he was the sort of guy who kicked cats and made kids cry. But the idea that he wished she'd called him ruggedly handsome instead irritated him. He almost wished she would tell him he rocked her world. That was a whole lot better than *kind* and blatant flattery would expose her for the fraud she was.

Audrey looked around and said, "I think you two can handle this. I'm going to wrap Val's presents."

J.P. glanced at his watch. "It's eleven-thirty. You've only got about five hours until her family party tonight. Are you sure that's enough time?"

"Smart aleck," she scolded, then laughed. "But it's

true there are a lot of gifts. If I can't get it done, I'll holler for reinforcements," she said on her way out of the room. She stopped in the doorway. "J.P., actually there is a rather large present I could use your help with."

He looked at Jane. "Are you all right?"

"Of course."

Other than being a fraudulent amnesiac. "I'll be back in a few minutes."

"Take your time."

Twenty minutes later, J.P. walked back into the great room to find Jane up on the ladder he'd brought in earlier. She was attaching the banner she'd finished to the two sconces on either side of the mantel.

"You should have waited for me," he said from behind her.

She was leaning sideways and started when he spoke. With a small shriek, she dropped the corner of the paper she was holding. Then she tried to grab it and lost her balance. J.P. reached up and caught her in his arms.

"My hero," she said, a little breathlessly. "I'm such a klutz."

"Is that an occupational hazard?"

"Probably. But it's partly your fault. You should make more noise when you come into a room. You startled me."

J.P. set her on her feet, his hands resting on her waist to steady her. Standing this close to her was dangerous, but he was oddly reluctant to let her go. The scent of her filled his head. Curves that had been keeping him awake nights were within his reach. Ever since that day he'd found her practically on his doorstep, the other time he'd caught her in his arms, he'd tried to erase the memory of her softness pressed against him.

Jane stepped away from him and picked up one of the pink balloons. Her hand was shaking. She met his gaze and shadows filled her own. Did she feel it, too, the tension arcing between them?

He took the end of the banner and stepped on the ladder. "I'll do this."

"You'll get no argument from me." She took one of the three dimensional bows she'd made from a roll of ribbon and tied the balloon to it. Then she turned away to attach it to the opposite side of the mantel from where he was working. "I know your niece's favorite color is pink, but it doesn't really go in this room."

"Is that your professional opinion?" His voice was hoarse, even to his own ears.

"Yes. Probably an instinctive thing. But we need to get our stories straight."

"Oh?" He knew she was in control of herself again when a corner of her mouth turned up.

She met his gaze. "When the interior decorator police raid the place, you've never seen me."

"Right. The reputation thing."

"It's everything in the business," she agreed.

"Well, at least you've remembered what you do. It's only a matter of time until you know who you are."

After attaching the banner to the sconce, he moved down the three steps and then moved the ladder aside. He watched her put the finishing touches on the bow and balloons that framed the mantel. She was wearing a floral jumper with a pale yellow, tailored T-shirt underneath. Her arms were toned and tan and the cotton material swirled around her, concealing more than it revealed. His fingers still tingled from the feel of her. The temptation to learn the exact size and shape of her curves twisted tight in his gut. The urge to taste her was almost irresistible.

But giving in to the attraction would be beyond stupid.

Just because he hadn't found a single chink in her cover didn't mean there wasn't one. It meant she was a brilliant con woman. Or her story—the coincidence of finding her on the street where he lived—was true. The fact that he could even consider the possibility meant that he was going crazy and she was driving him there.

And he'd brushed off his mother's suggestion to hire a private detective. That proved he on his way to certifiable.

It was proof of something else, too. He needed to get rid of Jane before he no longer cared if she made a fool of him.

Jordan was exhausted. It had been a long day what with ten little kids running around. Even with the ratio of kids to adults at two to one, she'd felt as if she were trying to harness a bevy of bees. When the little ones had left, the family celebration had begun. She liked J.P.'s sister and her husband. Their little girl was beyond adorable. Audrey didn't spoil her granddaughter. It was impossible to resist showering a child that cute with stuff.

Jordan was sitting outside on the patio swing, enjoying the peace and quiet of this beautiful September Texas evening. There was a pool and spa several feet away with redbrick decking surrounding them. The grounds of the estate were lovely. It was dark now, but during the day she knew there was grass spreading out as far as the eye could see. Trees, shrubs and flowers scattered here and there offset the stark landscape and added color. Wouldn't it be lovely to stay here forever? she thought dreamily.

"So this is where you escaped to."

Glancing to her right, Jordan saw J.P.'s sister standing beside the two-seater swing. Cathy O'Conner was a shorter, more delicate and very pregnant version of her brother. But apparently light on her feet in spite of her expanding waistline, since her approach had been silent.

"Care to join me? There's room for two in my escape module," she said.

"I'd love to."

Dark hair that barely brushed her shoulders and looked like silk swung forward as she sat in the empty space beside Jordan. A drink-holder console separated the two seats.

"What's everyone else doing?" Jordan asked.

"Kevin is in the kitchen with my mother, trying to convince her to let him set up a computer in her condo so she can do e-mail." She leaned back with a sigh. "And J.P. is playing with Val, showing her how to use the slot cars he wanted for himself."

Jordan laughed. "His niece is good cover for the latent kid in him."

"That's true. But Val sure responds to the kid in him. She adores her uncle." She glanced sideways. "By the way, thanks for all your help today."

"It was my pleasure. I enjoyed it," Jordan said.

"Mother told me what happened to you. I hope all the activity wasn't too much."

"Not at all."

Cathy rested her feet on the bricks and relaxed into the motion of the swing. "It must be strange not having memories."

Jordan squirmed. Getting even with J.P. was one thing. Deceiving the innocent people around him made her uncomfortable. She reminded herself it was for a just cause.

"It's weirder than you can imagine," she answered. It *would* be weird to have no memory. "But your mother has been so supportive. She's a real sweetheart." And Jordan sincerely meant that. "Nine out of ten people would have been anxious to get rid of me."

"Mom likes you, and her instincts about people are usually right on the money." Cathy shrugged. "That's good enough for me. But I bet J.P. is a different story."

"I can say with absolute honesty that I don't understand him at all."

The other woman laughed, but the humor was mixed with something darker. "He's got good reason to be cautious."

"He told me women throw themselves at him."

Leaning against the swing cushion, Cathy glanced sideways. "Yeah. But there was one particular woman who really did a number on him."

"Oh?"

Absently, Cathy rubbed her rounded belly. "Yeah. The one he proposed to was pregnant."

"Really? Since he's not married and I haven't heard about his children, I'm guessing there's more to this story."

"It gets really ugly."

"What happened?"

"I've never seen J.P. as happy as when he was engaged to Barbie Kiley. That's what fries my grits. He was so excited about the prospect of being a father. But she set him up from day one. The baby wasn't his."

"Uh-oh. How did he find out?" Jordan asked.

"The real father surfaced and blew the lid off the whole thing."

"She was marrying J.P. to give her baby a father?" Jordan guessed.

"That would have made her the tiniest bit noble, and, believe me, she wasn't. Like all the other women, she wanted my brother's money. But she had something none of them had."

"The baby." Jordan didn't know what to make of this information about the man she saw as an accessory to kidnapping. "How did he take the news?"

"He was devastated," Cathy said. "On many levels. She didn't want him for himself. The baby was another man's. J.P. found out practically at the altar, and he felt like a fool for falling into her trap. The wedding plans were big and splashy. When it all fell apart the humiliation was very public. But at least he didn't marry her."

Jordan stared at the other woman. She was describing a man who had a strict moral code and was capable of deep emotion. How could someone like that stoop to setting her up? It was no better than what Barbie Kiley had tried to do to him. "I don't know what to say."

"There isn't anything. I'm just afraid she hurt him so badly he'll never trust anyone. And he'll never be happy."

"I'm sure he'll get past it. He'll figure out a way

to find someone and settle down." If he hadn't already, Jordan thought.

Cathy smiled a little sadly. "I hope you're right. But I don't want him to wind up alone. A dotty old man rattling around in this huge castle. All he needs is a bunch of cats."

Jordan laughed. "You're exaggerating. I suspect J.P. can take care of himself."

"He can and does. By isolating himself. But he's so wonderful with Val. He'd be a wonderful father to his own children. It would be a tragedy if he never had any." There was a wry expression on her pretty face. "Kevin and Mother say I worry too much about him."

"Kevin and your mother are right." Jordan nodded toward her belly. "It seems to me that you've got enough to think about these days."

"No kidding. I am so ready to have this baby."

"When is it due?"

"Any day. Can't be too soon for me." She sighed. "And now I'm feeling guilty for hiding out. I better see what's going on with my daughter."

"I'll go with you." Jordan stood and waited.

Without moving, Cathy met her gaze. "I'm so huge, I just don't think I can get up without the assistance of heavy equipment."

"Yeah, right. You're so enormous," Jordan teased. When she held out her hand, the other woman took it, letting her assist her to her feet.

"Thanks," Cathy said, rubbing her lower back.

They walked back into the great room. J.P. was on the floor with his niece. He'd put together an intricate network of plastic track and now he was holding a control in his hand, manipulating the toggle switches to make the cars go faster or slower.

"I'm tired of cars, Uncle J.P." Valerie O'Conner was a blond, blue-eyed, curly-haired adorable moppet. "I want to try on the clothes Grandma got me."

"Okay." He sat up and looked at Jordan and his sister. "I thought I was going to have to send Search and Rescue to find you two."

"Just taking a break." Cathy put her hands on her hips. "You can store the slot cars here, J.P. Val won't mind if you play with them."

"I just might do that," he said, grinning up at her.

The little girl in question walked over to him with a shirt in each hand. "Uncle J.P.?"

"Munchkin?"

"Is tomorrow going to be an up-sleeve day or a down-sleeve day?"

Jordan leaned close to Cathy and whispered, "Care to translate that for me?"

"Short sleeves and long sleeves," the other woman whispered back.

"Ah." She watched J.P., fascinated by this side of him, especially after what his sister had revealed about his past.

He spread a pink shirt on one denim-clad thigh and a purple shirt on the other. Studying each as if it was a spreadsheet to net millions, he finally said, "I think you're probably going to want to go with up-sleeves."

"Goody." Val's curls bounced when she nodded. "That's the one I wanted to wear first."

"Is Kevin still in the kitchen with Mom?" Cathy asked.

J.P.'s hands looked too big as he carefully folded the tiny long-sleeved shirt. Finally, he looked up and said, "He figured if he started loading the birthday loot into the car he might finish by next Tuesday."

"You could help, you know," she shot back.

"I have orders from the birthday girl to keep playing. Your husband is an understanding guy. Or he's grateful for the backup. Either way I think he's a keeper, sis."

"He'd better be," she said, rubbing her belly. "He's going to be a father again any second."

Jordan was looking at J.P. and saw his reaction to the word *father*. A shadow hovered in his expression and his mouth pulled tight for a moment. Then the look was gone as suddenly as it had arrived.

He stood up. "In that case, I better help him."

"But, Uncle J.P., we're not finished playin'."

"I thought you wanted to put on a fashion show," he said.

"I want to play with my Polly Pocket stuff." She thrust her bottom lip out.

"She's so tired she doesn't know what she wants," Cathy said. "That means it's time to go home."

"I'm not tired. And I don't wanna go."

J.P. nodded and grabbed the little girl up in his arms. "I have an idea for a game. Let's play helping your father put all your presents in the car."

When he lifted Val onto his shoulders, she giggled. "I like being up high."

Jordan was impressed at the way he'd defused a potentially volatile situation. Fascinated, she watched him as he made trips back and forth, helping his niece carry the birthday booty. She and Audrey pitched in to make the job shorter. Cathy insisted on taking one present at a time. She said if physical labor would bring on childbirth then she was all for it.

Finally, their minivan was loaded to the rafters, Val was stowed in her car seat and they were ready to head home.

"Bye, Mom," Cathy said. "I'll call when there's something to report on the baby."

"Val will stay here with us when you go into labor," she said, hugging her daughter.

"I'm counting on it." Cathy kissed her mother and got in the car.

From the driver's side, Kevin bent slightly to look past his wife. "Bye, everyone. Thanks for everything, J.P."

"Any time."

Then the van moved down the tree-lined drive. Audrey stood between Jordan and J.P. as they watched until the red taillights disappeared. The stone entryway was lighted with coach lights on either side of the door. Spotlights discreetly placed in the shrubs cast semicircles of light on the castle walls.

"Unlike my granddaughter, I freely admit I'm exhausted." She sighed. "It's time for bed. Good night, you two."

"'Night," Jordan said.

"Sleep well, Mom."

She went inside, and Jordan was alone with J.P. Alone and confused. Will the real J. P. Patterson please stand up, she wanted to say. There was the uncle, brother and son who was a sweetheart. Then there was the underhanded creep who'd conspired with her father to kidnap and rescue her so she'd fall in love with him. After his devastating engagement experience, she almost couldn't blame him for attempting to control his love life. Almost.

But that still didn't explain why he hadn't made a

move on her since he'd brought her home. He was certainly taking his sweet time.

She glanced up. The twinkling stars made the sky look like black velvet sprinkled with glitter. "Nice night."

He folded his arms over his chest. "Yeah. I think the cold front finally got here to cool things off."

Maybe it was time to seize the day—or in this case night—and find out what would happen if *she* came on to *him*.

Rubbing her hands up and down her arms, she said, "It is a little chilly."

"Maybe you should go inside."

"What about you?"

He shrugged. "The air feels good."

She looked up at him, way up. The coach light on the stone castle wall behind him highlighted his wide shoulders and lean hips. His arms were folded over his broad chest, body language that wasn't especially inviting. She sized him up and wondered just how a girl went about the logistics of hitting on a guy. She'd never done it before. It would be easy for him. All he had to do was bend over and kiss her. The thought of it made her pulse skip.

"It does feel good," she agreed. "Just a little chilly."

If he was any kind of masher, wouldn't he take the hint and warm her up? Didn't he get that it was an invitation? A muscle contracted in his lean cheek, and his square jaw looked as hard and unforgiving as the stone walls of his castle. She'd taken a slew of classes in college, but not one of them had included techniques for kissing a man or Seduction 101.

"Here goes nothing," she mumbled.

''What?''

Awkwardly, she moved in front of him, close. Then she stood on tiptoe, but couldn't quite reach his mouth. She lifted her arms and took his face between her hands, savoring the sandpapery, masculine feel of his five o'clock shadow.

''What are you doing?'' he asked, his voice deep, husky.

''If you have to ask, my inexperience is showing.''

This was humiliating, but it was time to call his bluff. Get this show on the road and their cards on the table. She felt him tense and thought he was going to step away, but he didn't. Then she urged his head down and touched her lips to his. At first she felt his hesitation. Then one of his arms came around her and molded her against him. He slid his other hand into her hair, making the contact of their mouths more firm.

Feeling the heat of his big, warm body was like coming in from the cold. She hadn't expected that. When he traced the seam of her lips with his tongue, Jordan opened to him—a silent invitation to take whatever he wanted.

When he took, her senses scattered. A moment later they regrouped and focused on the exact place where he was touching the tip of his tongue to the corner of her mouth. A fire started deep and low in her belly, spreading heat outward.

He tasted good, really good, like something she hadn't known she'd been missing—until now. She breathed in the spicy, masculine scent of him and it went straight to her head like whiskey on an empty stomach. She felt dizzy and rested her hands on his chest, trying to get her balance. Her fingers curled into the fabric of his shirt as her tongue curved around his, darting, dueling, demanding.

When she slid her hand over his abdomen, he groaned low in his throat. The sound sent shock waves vibrating through her, setting off a hunger that she'd never felt before. She pulled her mouth from his, astonished at the thought. And a little bit frightened.

Jordan put her hand on his chest and felt his heart hammering beneath her palm. Pressing slightly, she was relieved when he lowered his arms and was no longer touching her. After drawing in air, she let it out slowly, trying to slow her pulse rate.

"Wow," she said.

"Ditto," he answered, his voice ragged and his breathing heavy.

He'd felt it, too. She knew he had. Hers had been spontaneous combustion. But how could that be?

This man was her father's lackey. Harman Bishop had picked him. That was strike one. J.P. had conspired with her father in order to manipulate her affections. That was strike two. But she'd seen another dimension to him. He was also good to his mother and wonderful with small children. And he wasn't a troll. She almost wished he were. That would make strike three and he would be out. He should be out anyway. But she felt a powerful attraction arcing between them and it made no sense.

"I hope you don't think I was throwing myself at you," she said, appalled at the breathlessness in her voice.

"Even though you were."

"Seemed a shame to waste such a beautiful night."

He looked at her, his eyes dark, unreadable. "I expected a response more along the lines of you couldn't help yourself.''

That was the first thing that had come to her mind. It *would* be her response if she didn't think of something else to say fast. ''I don't expect you to believe this, but I'm pretty sure I've never done anything like that before.''

''I kind of figured.''

Ever since she'd met him, her main focus had been to get the goods on him. But after tonight, learning about his past, Jordan's curiosity was piqued and she realized she wanted to get to know him better.

She backed up a step. ''J.P., I—''

''Yes?''

''Actually, I was wondering. What does J.P. stand for?''

He ran his fingers through his hair as he let out a long breath, as if he was relieved to have something innocuous to talk about. ''It stands for Jonathan Prince.''

She blinked at him. ''Your middle name is Prince?''

''Yeah. It's a family surname on my mother's side. My father's name was Jonathan, too. I got the initials to distinguish between us.''

His middle name was Prince? And he lived in a palace—castle. Jordan remembered that weird night in New Orleans with her friends, Rachel Manning and Ashley Gallagher. Rachel had wished for a baby, and now she had one. Ashley had wished for money and power, and she'd gotten both. Jordan had wished to be a princess and live in a palace. If J.P. was a Prince, did that mean whoever married him would be a Princess? Could this have anything to do with her wish? That was just plain nuts.

And so was she. To think kissing him would be the answer to her predicament. It had merely compounded everything. She was going soft, and she couldn't afford to do that. This time it was kidnapping. Next time she could be someone's sex slave. She couldn't live on the edge, wondering what mayhem her father would inflict next. He had to be stopped.

The only way to do that was to keep up the charade. At least she thought so, and kissing J.P. didn't make thinking any easier. She was so confused. She actually liked J.P. And that complicated the heck out of her plan.

Chapter Seven

"**J.P.,** the stock market crashed. Patterson, Inc. has lost everything. And I'm running away to Tahiti with my twenty-year-old boy toy."

"That's nice, Mother."

J.P. read the same paragraph in the newspaper for the fifth time and still couldn't remember what it said. He couldn't concentrate. Lack of sleep was partly responsible. And he hadn't slept much because he couldn't forget how beautiful Jane had looked in the moonlight. Or how sweet her mouth had tasted. Or that her curvy little body had felt like sin pressed against his own.

"Jonathan Prince Patterson, you're not listening to me."

He looked across the kitchen table. Audrey didn't use all three of his names very often. When she did, he knew it was time to crank up all of his brain cells and focus on what she was saying instead of thinking about the fascinating things moonlight did to Jane's eyes. "What makes you think I wasn't listening, Mother?"

"It was the boy-toy remark."

"What boy toy?"

"I don't have one." She sighed. "But an old woman can always hope."

"Over my dead body."

"You're doing a pretty good imitation of that right now. You didn't hear a word I said. What's wrong with you?"

Besides kissing Jane Doe and having the frustrated sexual response to prove it? "Not a darn thing."

Audrey took a sip of coffee, then set her china cup on the matching saucer in front of her without ever taking her gaze from his. "Ever since you were a little boy and you first started talking, I could always tell when you were lying."

"How?" he asked, trying to blank out any expression that would tip her off to his inner turmoil.

"It's nothing overt like your eyes cross or twitch. Or a pronounced stutter. Just a general thing. A mom thing. Does this mood of yours have anything to do with Jane?" She pointed at him. "And if you lie to me again, I'll know it."

He closed the newspaper, knowing between his determined mother and his lack of concentration, he couldn't read it anyway. "All right. Yes. My mood has something to do with Jane."

"I knew it." She folded her hands and leaned forward. "What's the scoop? Do you have feelings for her?"

"You could say that."

"Don't be clever, J.P. I'm talking about romantic feelings. Do you like her?"

"I don't know if I'd go that far."

"But you're not unaffected by her." It wasn't a question.

"That's safe to say."

"I knew it. I saw you kiss her last night." She met his gaze and hers was completely unapologetic. "I peeked out the parlor window."

The muscle in his jaw twitched as he clenched his teeth. When he could respond in a normal tone he said, "You were spying on me? For crying out loud, Mother."

"So sue me. But it was quite obvious from my vantage point that there were sparks between you and Jane when you kissed."

"In all honesty I can say she started it."

And that's what puzzled him the most. She was a good kisser, once he'd taken charge of the situation. But her initial attempt was clumsy and unpracticed. He'd expected more from an experienced swindler. But it was the strangest thing. He liked her better for her awkwardness. Except he couldn't say for sure that it wasn't part of her act. And that, in a nutshell, was why he was distracted this morning.

"You sound like a ten-year-old tattling on your sister."

Jane was no child and most assuredly *not* his sister. "It's nothing more than the truth."

"I think you liked kissing Jane," his mother guessed. "I think you're attracted to her."

"I'm not saying you're right. But it makes no sense. I don't know anything about her."

"Chemistry isn't based on intimate knowledge," Audrey pointed out. "You don't need to know her life history to know she turns you on."

"Oh, for Pete's sake, Mother."

"It's true. And don't scold. I'm old, not dead. I think you've got the hots for Jane and it scares you."

"Can you blame me? That fiasco with Barbie is proof that my judgment leaves a lot to be desired."

"That woman should rot in hell for using her baby to trap you into marriage and get her hands on your money." Her mouth thinned. "God knows I'd like to cut her heart out with a spoon, but not all women are like her. There are good ones out there."

"The problem is how do you know the difference?"

"Instinct. Mine tells me Jane is a good one."

"Again I say you don't know anything about her. And she won't or can't tell us because of her memory loss."

"In all the books—"

He held up his hand to stop her. "Movies, romance novels and soap operas are not real life."

"Maybe not. But amnesia only blocks memories. It doesn't alter the true nature of a person. Jane is warm-hearted and caring. Did you see her with the children yesterday? They loved her. She was funny and energetic and I don't know what we'd have done without her since Cathy is in no shape to help. Kids especially can't be fooled. If she was a phony, they'd have spotted it a mile away."

"I don't know. What if she's married? Jane, I mean."

"I knew that. But I don't think she is. No ring. And no tan line showing she ever wore one on her left ring finger."

"Still, Mom—"

She reached over and patted his hand. "Something

traumatic happened to her, J.P. I'm sure of it. She's telling the truth about that. If she wasn't, I'd know it."

"You're sure?"

"Absolutely," she said, nodding emphatically. "She's very lucky you came along when you did."

Jordan heard Audrey's remark as she walked into the kitchen. Obviously they were discussing the day he'd found her on the road—the day that turned her life upside down.

"Good morning," she said.

"Jane, dear," Audrey said. "We were just talking about you."

"Really?" She looked directly at J.P.

He leaned back in his chair and stared at her measuringly. "Mother was just saying that the kidnapping was traumatic for you."

"It was," she agreed, shivering as she remembered her initial fear. "I don't ever want to go through anything like that again."

"Of course you don't, dear. As soon as your memory returns you can tell the sheriff everything and catch the person who did this."

"That's just it. Nothing seems to be happening on the memory front." That wasn't a complete lie. "And there's no sign it will. I can't help feeling as if I've imposed on you long enough. I think it's time for me to go."

Audrey looked distressed. "You don't mean that."

Jordan had never meant anything more. She'd tossed and turned most of the night thinking about J.P.—Jonathan *Prince* Patterson. The man lived in a castle, for goodness' sake. This scenario was like some crackpot Aladdin genie's idea of a practical joke. It was too much like what she'd wished for. And she happened to know that Rachel and Ashley had gotten what they'd wished for—in a fractured-fairy-tale sort of way. Because of their whacked-out wishes come true, they'd fallen in love and were engaged to be married.

But this was the thing. Jordan didn't want this wish—not if it included J.P. Even if she could reconcile the fact that he'd been a coconspirator in the kidnapping, he was a workaholic like her father. The woman who married him would be nothing more than an afterthought, an asterisk in his life. She'd seen her mother go through that and it wasn't going to happen to her. That meant putting the brakes on any attraction to him. Her only option was to run far and fast. It was time for her to leave.

"I'm not your problem. I think it would be best if J.P. takes me into town to the sheriff."

"Of course we'll help you any way we can. But—" Audrey's face clearly showed her disappointment.

Jordan felt like the slimy underside of a lake-bottom rock. "You've been more kind than I deserve."

"Nonsense. But I'm not sure leaving is best. I just can't bear the idea that essentially you have nowhere to go."

"The sheriff can point me in the direction of assistance," she said.

"But what about the progress you've made since being here? You're an interior designer." She tapped her lip thoughtfully. "J.P. has mentioned redecorating this place."

"I have?"

Audrey shot him a go-with-me-on-this glance. "I'm sure you were thinking about it. And your office. It hasn't been redone since way before your father died.

It's past time to make changes there. Jane, I really do think that getting back to work might stir things up and perhaps bring some of your memories to the surface.''

Jordan groaned inwardly as she twisted her fingers together. This was killing her. The woman was such a dear. She should just confess. Right here, right now. Get it out in the open. The only thing stopping her was disappointing Audrey. Forcing her to see that her son could be involved in such an underhanded, nefarious, twisted plot.

She shook her head. ''I don't know—''

Audrey settled her cloth napkin on the table beside her china cup and saucer. ''If putting you back in your work element doesn't do the trick, we'll find another way. Right, J.P.?''

He nodded. ''We could always hire a private detective to check into your background. I'll hire someone myself.''

He'd eighty-sixed that idea the first time it came up. What was his game now, Jordan wondered. ''And you'd be all right with me making changes here in the castle and at your office?''

He shrugged. ''It's for a good cause. If I can help—''

''You're a good man, J.P.'' Audrey beamed at him.

''A real hero.'' One corner of his mouth quirked up. ''To the rescue again.''

Jordan stiffened at the words—*hero, rescue*. She would never think of them in quite the same white-knight light ever again. Not after that awful day she'd been grabbed and bullied and terrified. She was still sore about her missing shoe. And this man was responsible. His words convinced her she couldn't leave yet. She had to try and get to the bottom of this.

And if she asked him point-blank, he would deny any part in the kidnapping. She'd give him just a little longer to show his true colors. With enough rope, surely he would hang himself. Then she'd take him down, embarrass him thoroughly until he'd want nothing to do with any of the Bishops. Once and for all she would put a stop to Harman Bishop's machinations.

"If you're sure—"

"We are," Audrey assured her.

"Then I'll stay," she agreed.

Two days later, Jordan was glad they'd talked her into staying. For Audrey's sake. Cathy had gone into labor during the night and first thing in the morning Kevin had taken her to the hospital after dropping Val off at the castle to stay with her grandmother. Not an hour later, the little girl had fallen down outside and cut her knee badly enough to need stitches.

And J.P. was at work. Shades of Jordan's father.

Audrey had tried to get ahold of him. She'd called his cell number. After getting voice mail, she'd phoned his secretary and been told he was in a very important meeting and couldn't be disturbed. His mother had said if the woman valued her job, she would interrupt that meeting and tell him his sister was having a baby and there was a good chance his niece needed stitches. They would be at the hospital. Then she'd hung up.

The emergency room doctor had confirmed that because of the location of the injury and to facilitate healing, the little girl did need a couple stitches in her knee. After hearing that, Audrey had insisted a plastic surgeon do the procedure. If she'd been a boy, a scar would be cool. But she wasn't. Hence, they were waiting for the specialist in reconstructive surgery to arrive.

Because Jordan was there to stay with Val, Audrey had gone upstairs to Labor and Delivery to inform the child's father what was going on. While Audrey stayed with Cathy, Kevin had come down to see for himself that Val was basically all right and give permission for her treatment. Now Audrey was going back and forth between the E.R. and Labor and Delivery.

At the moment, Val was sitting in Jordan's lap. The child's leg was stretched out straight with a small sterile disposable drape covering the deep wound. Because the little girl had been so upset by the unfamiliar medical setting, they all decided she'd be more comfortable in the waiting area as opposed to a trauma room until the doctor arrived to do the procedure. They were watching a cartoon program on the TV mounted on the wall.

"You hanging in there, sweetie?" Jordan asked, rubbing her arm.

"I wanna go home." She settled her head against Jordan's chest.

"You're being very brave," Jordan whispered past the lump in her own throat.

"That's what my daddy said." She heaved a big sigh. "It sure is taking a long time."

"I know. They had to find the doctor, and he's driving here—"

"No. I mean it's taking a long time for my mommy to get my baby sister."

"What if your mommy has a boy baby?"

"I don't want a brother. I asked for a sister."

Jordan had, too, once upon a time. She'd hated being an only child and resolved if she ever found the right guy, she'd have half a dozen kids. At least Val would have a sibling. Jordan's parents hadn't had any more babies. She found she liked the feel of this small body in her arms.

Jordan brushed the child's blond curls off her forehead. "Even if your mommy has a boy, you'll still be the big sister. You can play with him."

"But boys can't play with dolls."

"Says who?"

"I don't 'member."

"If he wants to, he can," Jordan pointed out. "Just like you played slot cars with your Uncle J.P."

"Yeah. It was fun," Val agreed.

"See? And a baby brother might think it's fun to play house. When he's old enough, he might even want to be the daddy."

The child thought about that. "Like my daddy plays with me."

"Just like that."

"Mommy says I should be a good 'zample to my baby brother or sister. Like Uncle J.P. was to her."

Now Cathy's big brother was all grown up. He was a man. Jordan shivered as she remembered how good it had felt to be sheltered in his strong arms. But he was a man to whom business had become more important than the needs of his family. Audrey was running herself ragged and he couldn't be bothered to help.

Jordan rubbed her cheek against the child's hair. "I'm sure whether your mommy has a boy or girl, you're going to be an excellent big sister."

Just then the E.R. doors whispered open and a man walked in. Hoping it was the plastic surgeon, Jordan looked up. It was J.P.

He'd discarded his suit coat and rolled up the sleeves of his white dress shirt. His geometric-patterned silk tie in shades of green and gold had been loosened. He stood there looking around frantically and started toward the reception desk where they'd registered after bringing Val in.

The little girl in her lap sat up. "Uncle J.P. I'm over here."

"Val?" He turned to look, then hurried to her and squatted down in front of them. "Hi, munchkin. Are you okay?"

"I hurt my knee," she said, her voice trembling.

"That's what I heard."

"A doctor's comin' to make it better." The child thrust her lower lip out.

When he looked at Jordan for an explanation, she said quietly, "Audrey insisted on a plastic surgeon to do the repair. He's on his way."

J.P. nodded. "Where's my mother?"

"She went upstairs to check on Cathy."

"Any news yet about the baby?" he asked.

"It's gonna be a sister," Val said.

One of his eyebrows rose in question. "What if it's a boy?"

"We just had this conversation," Jordan said. "I think I've persuaded her that when he's old enough he's capable of playing anything she wants. Even the daddy if they play babies."

He nodded. "Excellent negotiation."

"Wanna see my boo-boo, Uncle J.P.?"

"Do I?" he asked, his grin fading as he met Jordan's gaze.

"It's quite an impressive boo-boo," she said, trying to warn him without frightening the little girl.

He gingerly lifted the sterile drape by one corner, then turned pale as he studied the wound. "That is impressive."

"I fell on a sprinkler," Val said. "I was twirling around in your yard, and I got dizzy. But I didn't see the sprinkler."

"I'm sorry you hurt yourself. But the doctor will make it all better soon." He reached out as if he needed to touch Val. Then he hesitated, studying her, obviously not wanting to add to her discomfort.

"If you want to hold her," Jordan said, "I think I can give her to you without jostling her leg too much."

"Val, do you want to sit with me?" J.P. asked.

She shook her head. "Wanna stay with Jane. Don't wanna move my leg. It might bleed some more."

"Okay," he said, shoving his fingers through his hair.

"I thought you were in a meeting," Jordan said, making small talk.

"I was."

"Your secretary said you couldn't be disturbed."

"That's standard secretary speak. But she has orders to put through any communication from my family."

"What happened to the meeting?"

He met her gaze. "It ended as soon as my secretary gave me Mother's message."

Jordan saw the tension in his jaw and the muscle contracting in his cheek. He was concerned. Not only was he concerned, he'd ended a business meeting on account of the situation going on with his family. She looked into his face and had the most absurd desire to reach out and smooth the worry lines from his forehead. Her heart skipped once, and she took a deep breath to fortify herself against the sensation. She didn't quite know what to do with the information that he was a caring man who put everything aside for family. What an amazing thing.

He glanced over his shoulder to the reception desk. "I think I'll see what's holding up that doctor."

He stood and Jordan watched him move purposefully toward the receptionist. His voice carried as he quietly, but forcefully and authoritatively asked questions to assess the situation. He was impressive and her heart swelled, sending a feeling of tenderness coursing through her. How great was this? A man to run interference and maybe get some action. A warrior fighting for the ones he loved. Her warm, fuzzy feeling became a dangerous and very disturbing thing when she realized how very, very glad she was that he was there.

He walked back. "The doctor's here and setting things up in the trauma room. The nurse is going to call us back in a minute."

Val clutched Jordan's shirt. "I want Mommy."

"I know, sweetie. And your mommy would like to be here, but she's having a baby. You have Uncle J.P. And your grandma. And I'll stay with you if you want." Jordan tucked her hair behind her ear.

"Do you want Grandma?" J.P. asked. "I'll go get her."

The little girl looked up at him with her big solemn eyes, then glanced at Jordan. "I think maybe Mommy needs Grandma. Can you and Jane go in the room with me, Uncle J.P.?''

''Sure,'' he said and a little more color washed out of his face.

Something told Jordan he would rather sell short on the stock market than watch this little girl go through anything painful.

When the nurse finally called them, J.P. took the child into his strong arms and carried her back, gently setting her on the sheet-draped gurney. As the staff readied her for the procedure, he held her hand. Then he took Jordan's with his other. Even warriors needed a source of strength, she thought. Heat spread through her, warming her insides like caramel left in the sun too long.

The doctor explained what he was going to do, and Val started crying quietly.

J.P. squeezed Jordan's hand tighter. ''Look at me, munchkin. Like the doctor said, a little pinch and it won't hurt anymore.''

''Don't go away, Uncle J.P. Stay with me.''

He smiled tenderly. ''There's nowhere else I'd rather be.''

''We should try to distract her,'' Jordan said.

''How?'' he asked, glancing at her.

How, indeed. It wasn't like they could do handstands or play with toys. All they had were words. ''Would you like a story?''

Val's troubled, teary gaze met her own. ''Like you told at my party?''

''Just like that.'' When the child solemnly nodded, Jordan said, ''Once upon a time there was a little princess named Valerie—''

''Me?'' she said.

"You," Jordan answered.

She whimpered when the doctor numbed the area with an injection from a tiny needle. But the medication must have worked quickly because almost immediately she quieted and looked at Jordan.

"What happened to the princess?" she asked.

"Princess Valerie had a baby brother. He was crying all the time," she said. "So the princess decided to figure out a way to make him laugh."

Jordan didn't know where the words came from, but she said anything that came to mind. Apparently the pacing of her story was adequate because it held the child's attention while the doctor took the tiniest possible stitches to minimize any scarring on her leg. When he finished, he gave them instructions and a prescription for pain meds if she needed any.

J.P. handled all the paperwork, then while Jordan stayed with the little girl, he went upstairs to inform his mother and sister that everything was fine. When he walked out of the elevator to take them home, Jordan's heart did that funny little skip that she now knew meant she was glad to see him. Glad to see him? A pathetic little phrase to describe the magnitude of her feelings.

"How's Cathy?" Jordan asked.

"She's fully dilated and they're taking her to delivery," he said. "Mom's going to stay because her doctor says it shouldn't be long now."

Jordan nodded. "Okay."

"The car is waiting." He looked at his niece. "The nurse is going to take you outside in a chair with wheels."

"Can we go fast?" the little girl wanted to know.

"Not too fast. And no wheelies," he said, his mouth quirking up.

"Okay. Are you coming home with Jane and me?"

"I am," he answered.

"What about your meeting?" Jordan asked.

"It's been rescheduled. Some things are more important."

And those simple words convinced Jordan that she was in very, very big trouble.

Chapter Eight

In a foul mood, J.P. walked into his office after the fiasco of the rescheduled meeting. Jane was standing with her back to the doorway and one of his yellow legal pads in her hands. She seemed deep in thought as she looked around, then jotted something down. She was wearing a beige linen skirt with a sleeveless, silky cream-colored blouse that left her toned arms bare. The matching jacket was draped over the high back of one of the tufted leather wing chairs in front of his desk.

He was still seething from the meeting. Until he walked in and saw Jane, he'd forgotten all about her, including the fact that she'd accompanied him today to evaluate his office for redecoration. When he thought of the tough negotiator he'd left behind, he could almost feel his blood pressure spike. But the sight of Jane seemed an antidote and sent his pressure upward—in a good way. The soft, bare flesh of her arms sent his thoughts in a direction where she was pretty much bare all over. Did she have tan lines from her bathing suit? Bikini or tank? The wondering made him hot all over and sent his thoughts in yet another direction—his bed, with twisted sheets and tangled limbs.

The good news was he couldn't maintain his foul frame of mind at the same time he was appreciating how beautiful she was. The bad news—his reaction meant he was attracted to this woman. Right, wrong or indifferent, he liked her a lot and had acknowledged it to himself two days ago when his nephew was born.

Jane had pitched in during the crisis without hesitation. She'd been steady as the Rock of Gibraltar during Val's stitches when he'd been ready to keel over. Her calm demeanor had set the bar so high he simply wouldn't let himself fall apart. Being surrounded by calm adults had reassured his niece, who was home now with her new baby brother.

"Hi," he said, leaning a shoulder against the door frame.

Jane whirled around, and the expression on her face clearly showed she was startled. "I didn't hear you come in."

"Yet here I am." He would guess she liked her profession if she could so successfully tune out everything around her. He loved running his company, but he wasn't sure if he would be unaware of her presence if she stood watching him. In fact, he remembered the morning not so long ago when he'd tried to work in the library at the castle and knew the exact moment she'd entered the room.

He straightened away from the wall and moved farther into his office. "What do you think of the place?"

"Your mother's right. It could use a face-lift."

He glanced around. "I haven't changed anything since taking over after my dad passed away."

"How long ago was that?"

"Almost two years now. I still miss him," he added, then wondered why. No reason except something about Jane made sharing easy.

"I recommend pictures and keepsakes. And telling stories of your memories to his grandchildren. Sharing the kind of man he was with them is an excellent method of keeping his memory alive. As opposed to keeping his office a dusty, dated shrine."

"Are you being a smart aleck?"

"Only about the dusty, dated shrine part." She grinned. "Speaking of grandchildren, I talked to Audrey and she said Val continues to be a brave little soldier about her stitches and little Tyler Paul is holding up like the sturdy newborn he is."

"Yeah. I called Cathy. Good to know things are getting back to normal at the same time you're going to turn my world upside down." That comment was way too close to another personal revelation. So he added, "Here at work. Redecorating."

Her dark eyes glowed with excitement. "I have some wonderful ideas. Would you like to hear them?"

"Yes." Her wide smile seared all the way to his soul. He wanted anything she could dish out to take his mind off the temptation to pull her into his arms and kiss her.

She stood beside him and surveyed the area. "I think you need a new desk. That may be sacrilege since that's your father's. But you need something to better accommodate a computer. There's a lovely little niche in one of the castle's upstairs bedrooms where this would fit perfectly, so you'd have it as a keepsake.''

"Okay."

"The sofa against the wall is in good shape, but it badly needs a change. I suggest recovering it in a chenille fabric or a cotton twill. Both are comfortable, cozy and have a lot of eye appeal. Some overstuffed throw pillows in bold shades to bring out the muted wheat color of the walls will make the room pop. And wooden shutters instead of blinds and curtains. I like white, but an oak shade would work, too. And it's more masculine.''

As she studied the room, she absently tapped her pen against her mouth. Lucky pen, he thought. And speaking of popping—

"What do you think?" she asked.

"Hmm?" He looked at her and took a deep breath to calm his hammering heart. "I think it sounds great."

"Are you sure?" she said, studying him now. "I didn't mean to make light of your feelings about your father. If you think it's too soon to make changes, I—"

He touched a finger to her lips to silence her. "I took steps to deal with it. I have to tell you, redecorating his office would have been a lot less traumatic than what I did.''

She blinked up at him, surprise evident in her eyes. "What does that mean? Did you pierce your eyebrow? Go bungee jumping off the San Francisco Bay bridge? Skydiving over Kansas?"

"None of the above." He rubbed the back of his neck. "I got engaged."

"To Barbie?"

"Yes," he said, wincing at the sarcasm in her tone. "It was right after Dad died. My mother, the amateur analyst who received her training from soap operas and romance novels, has a theory."

"And what would that be?" Jane said with a smile.

"She says I was probably drawn to the woman and the child she said was mine because of some deep need to reaffirm life after losing someone as important to me as my father."

"It makes sense."

"Or there could be another truth."

"Which is?" she asked.

"That I'm simply a gullible moron."

She shook her head. "I don't buy that. You're not simple, gullible or a moron."

"Thank you."

That warmed him clear to his bruised and battered soul. At the same time it made him nervous. At best, his judgment was questionable. So how could he not question his incredible attraction to this woman he knew so little about? But at least he had two things going for him. His mother liked her and so did his niece. Val had never taken to his fiancé. Barbie had tried bribes of food and gifts yet nothing worked. But Val had taken to Jane immediately and no buy-off had been involved.

A flush spread over her cheeks as she met his gaze, then she blinked and looked away. "So how did the meeting go?"

And the spell was broken as his anger over the encounter kicked in again. J.P. ran his hand through his hair. "Could have been better."

She looked at him, with what appeared to be genuine concern on her face. "What's the problem?"

"One of my competitors is liquidating parts of his company. I'm in negotiations to buy them."

"That doesn't sound problematic."

"It is when the seller doesn't know the meaning of *compromise* or *negotiation*. He wants everything his own way and doesn't care who he has to walk on to get it. That's not the way I do business. I expect to pay a fair price, but no one is going to stick it to me."

She turned her back to the room and leaned against one of the chairs in front of his desk. "I'm pretty sure I know nothing about the business of mergers and acquisitions."

"What makes you think that?"

"Because," she hesitated as if she were searching for the right words. "When I was looking at this office I was thinking color, fabric, sizzle, pop and swatches. That felt right." She folded her arms beneath her breasts. "But compromise and negotiation sounds completely unfamiliar."

"And what's your point?" He was pretty sure she had one. Because in the time he'd known her, he'd learned she always did.

"My point is that if you're so repelled by the man and his tactics, why don't you back out of the whole thing?"

"Because I've already spent a lot of man-hours and money on this deal."

"So what?" She shrugged. "If you're not going to get what you want, is it worth all the aggravation? Is this deal, or lack of a deal, going to put you out of business? Or am I simplifying the situation too much?"

Her words sank in. The more he thought about it, the more he liked what she'd said. He took one step forward, closing the gap between them and wrapped his fingers around her upper arms. He pulled her against him and said, "You're brilliant."

Then he lowered his mouth to hers. Her surprise instantly evaporated into a sigh of pleasure. Her palms rested on his chest, and he could feel the heat through his shirt.

J.P. slid one hand to her waist, encircling it with his arm as he snuggled her to him with a sigh he simply couldn't suppress. The feel of her soft curves nestled against his hard length fueled the banked fire inside him. He nuzzled her neck and inhaled deeply to savor the sweet scent of her skin. The sparks dancing through him burst into flame.

He traced the seam of her lips with his tongue and she instantly opened to admit him. Tasting the honeyed interior of her mouth trapped the breath in his lungs. Holding her like this made him feel as if he could hardly breathe. And he couldn't find the will to care.

She broke off the kiss and stared up at him, breathing hard. "I'm glad you think I'm brilliant," she added. "But I don't understand what I said to give you that impression."

He couldn't quite remember either. His mental processes had ceased as soon as he'd touched the bare flesh of her arms. It seemed his blood flow had gone south instead of circulating through his brain.

He kissed the tip of her nose, then stepped away for the distance necessary to form a coherent thought. After dragging in a deep breath, he said, "You're correct. It's not as simple as it sounds to just walk away from the deal."

"Okay. But I still don't get how I was brilliant."

"If I make noises about calling off the deal, Harman Bishop will change his tone."

"Who?"

"Harman Bishop. He's the most difficult, stubborn, opinionated, dogged man I've ever dealt with. Some sources say he's unprincipled as well. So far I haven't seen that side of him. But at this point I wouldn't put anything past him. He's a shark, and I want to beat him at his own game."

"I—I see."

"And you just gave me the strategy I need."

Jordan told J.P. she needed more time alone in his office to evaluate the decor and think about changes. What was one more fib? He obliged her, since he had some things to do away from his desk. As soon as she was alone, she plopped herself into his cushy chair, picked up his phone and got an outside line. Then she dialed her father's cell phone number.

After one and a half rings he answered. "Hello," he barked.

"Daddy—"

"Jordan? Where the hell are you? Are you all right?"

Was that genuine concern in his voice? It warmed her heart while at the same time she wanted to wring his neck. "I'm fine."

"Thank God. I've been worried sick."

"Really?"

"Of course. No one's heard from you. They found your purse on the ground by your car at my office."

"And my shoe?"

"What about your damn shoe?"

"I lost it. In the struggle with the thug-in-training you hired to grab me."

On the other end of the line, the silence spoke volumes. "What are you talking about? A thug I hired?"

So he was going to try to brazen it out. That was no more than she'd expected. "It's over, Dad. I know what you did. It's amazing the information one can acquire from a well-placed knee to the groin followed a few minutes later by a no-holds-barred ear yank."

There was another long silence, and she could almost hear the wheels of his mind turning.

"What do you know?"

"Everything. Now I want to hear your side. And before you start, Daddy, I know you're behind this kidnapping. So I strongly advise you to tell me the truth."

"Okay. You win," he growled. After a heavy sigh he said, "I hired one of the flunky college students who works for me to grab you that day you and I had lunch. His orders were to drive you around until you were disoriented then wait on a specific road."

"For my hero to rescue me?"

"Yeah."

"Then I would be so grateful I'd fall in love with the man of your choosing."

"Jordan, I'm your father. It's my responsibility to take care of you."

"And you've done a fine job of that so far," she said sarcastically.

"I'm not going to be around forever," he went on as if she hadn't spoken. "It's important to me that you're settled and taken care of, sweetheart."

"Don't you sweetheart me. Did you give a thought

to what I want?'' she demanded. ''Did it occur to you that this plan of yours was completely insane?''

''The plan was a good one. I don't understand what went wrong.''

''It was wrong from the beginning.''

''The kid said he dropped you off at the designated spot. Clark came by and—''

Good Lord, did he mean the man who'd put the *smarm* in *smarmy?* ''Please tell me you don't mean Clark Caldwell.''

''One and the same.'' Was there a note of irritation in his voice.

''He was late, Dad.''

''Just a few minutes he said—''

''We waited for a long time. After I got the drop on your flunky, he left me there on the road. Clark never showed. At least not while I was there.''

''He told me he had a flat and was only twenty minutes late. When he came, there was no sign of you or the flunky.'' His voice shook with emotion. ''I called the cops and told them everything.''

''Everything? Including the fact that you set me up?''

''Yeah.''

''I hope you were completely humiliated.''

''When they couldn't turn anything up,'' he continued, ignoring her remark, ''I hired a private investigator.''

''You did?'' He cared enough to suffer the humiliation of calling reinforcements to find her. She hated the way that information tugged at her heart, especially after what he'd put her through.

''Yeah, I did. No one could find a trace. Where the hell have you been all this time?''

Jordan was trying to wrap her mind around this. J.P. had come along and stopped. She'd assumed he was in on the kidnap plot. But his arrival was simply coincidence. He was as innocent in all of this as she was. Well, in her case, not so much. This was such a mess.

"Jordan? Are you still there?"

"Yes, Daddy."

"You're all right? It's been two weeks. You didn't have your purse. No money or credit cards. You were abandoned on the road. What the hell happened?"

"I was kidnapped," she said wryly.

"You know what I mean. Where are you? Where have you been? You're really all right?"

"Some very decent people took me in. I've been staying with the Pattersons." And deceiving them. She rubbed the pain starting to throb between her eyes as she leaned back in J.P.'s chair.

"Patterson? That wouldn't happen to be Audrey Patterson?"

"Yes." Interesting he'd mentioned her, Jordan thought. He'd just had a business meeting with J.P., yet he'd brought up his mother. "Do you know her?"

"Years ago. When she was Audrey Prince. That was before I met your mother and Audrey married someone else. She was a lovely woman."

"She still is," Jordan said, stomach knotting. "She took in a complete stranger who led her to believe she needed help."

"Why didn't you call me?" His tone was part exasperation, part desperation. "I'd have come for you."

"After what you did? It's your fault I had to rely on the kindness of strangers in the first place. You're out of control. It's got to stop, Daddy."

"Jordan, listen to me. I was thinking of you. I did it for you."

"That is so not true. You did it for you. So you wouldn't have to worry about me. At this moment, I can truthfully say I don't ever want to see or speak to you again."

"Jordan, listen—"

She heard J.P.'s voice in the outer office. "Goodbye, Daddy."

She hung up the phone feeling like the star in an episode of *I Love Lucy* gone bad. There were so many signs that she should have paid attention to—clues, hints, indications, suggestions that J.P. wasn't involved with this twisted scheme.

Completely miserable, she buried her face in her hands. No wonder he never made a move on her. Until today, she thought, her heart sinking. He'd tolerated her presence for his mother's sake. He'd been used, abused and emotionally burned by a woman who was only after his money. He wasn't inclined to let his guard down again. The really unfortunate thing was that she genuinely liked him. Even when she thought he was the one her father had set her up with she couldn't resist being drawn to him. In her ultimate arrogance, aka stupidity, she'd made a move on him. In spite of all that, today she'd gotten the feeling he really liked her, too. And now this.

"Please, God," she prayed. "Let the earth open now and just swallow me whole."

She put her arms on his desk and rested her forehead on them. The magnitude of the mess continued to wash over her, one tidal wave after another.

She lifted her head and looked around his office, remembering what had happened just a little while ago. He'd grabbed her and kissed her for all he was worth. That was a positive. Plus, he didn't like her father very much, which was something they had in common at the moment. Maybe this wasn't as bad as she thought.

All she had to do was explain to him why she'd done what she'd done, then it might be possible to salvage the relationship. And she found she very much wanted that. She *really* liked him a lot. Maybe more than like. Her instinct told her he was everything she'd always wanted.

The time had come to dig herself out of the hole her father had landed her in. Yes, she'd compounded the mess, but Harman Bishop had set the chain of events in motion. Unlike him, she would tell J.P. the truth. But considering how badly he'd been hurt, she had to find just the right words to make him understand.

She stood and squared her shoulders. Somehow, she would make it right.

Chapter Nine

J.P.'s office was halfway between Dallas and Sweet Spring, about thirty minutes from the estate. Usually he made the drive alone. He told himself he liked the solitude, and most of the time he did. But he liked having Jane beside him more, and he took his eyes off the road in front of him just long enough to glance over at her. That morning he'd enjoyed her company—reluctantly and against his better judgment. If he'd been able to control the sensation he would have, but he couldn't.

Her observations about people and places had made him laugh. Her comments were smart and sensible. Her curvy shape made his hands alternately tingle and itch to touch her. The memory of having her in his arms sent a shaft of heat straight to his groin. Her responsive, small, sexy moan when he'd kissed her said she was responding to *him*. J. P. Patterson the man, not the rich CEO.

He glanced over at her again. She'd hardly said two

words since he'd kissed her and that worried him. It wasn't like her to be quiet for this long. He'd been so caught up in the moment, the exhilaration of her simple strategy to deal with Harman Bishop, he'd just grabbed her and let it rip. But the truth was if it hadn't been that, he'd have found some other excuse to take her in his arms and kiss the living daylights out of her. She'd been acting weird ever since.

This silence was driving him up the wall. They were five minutes from the castle and he wanted the loquacious Jane back before they got there.

"Cat got your tongue?" he asked.

A very large sigh came from the passenger side of the vehicle. "Have you ever wondered where that expression came from?"

"Truthfully? No."

"Me, either. Until now. And it's pretty gross if you think about it."

"I suppose. But—"

She crossed one leg over the other. "The idea of a cat getting your tongue. How could one do that? If you take it that far, they only have paws. How would one hang on to it? That's where the concept gets really icky."

"Whoa. I didn't mean to start a philosophical discussion. I simply wondered why you're so quiet."

"Maybe I'm just a quiet person."

"All evidence to the contrary." He turned off the main road, stopped at the security gate and waited for it to open. When it did, he guided the SUV through and up the tree-lined drive.

She was really being reserved, and he didn't like it. But he really liked her. In spite of his warnings, somehow she'd sneaked past his defenses. Whatever her story was, somehow it didn't matter anymore. He no longer believed she was after his money.

His mother was right. A person's inner character shined through, and Jane's was sweet and smart and sexy. The rest would work itself out.

He realized now that women coming on to him for his money only partly bothered him. Because he could take care of that with a handy dandy thing called a prenuptial agreement. But he was just enough of a romantic to resist resorting to that. After Barbie, he'd never trusted that any woman cared about him for himself.

Until Jane. She was different; he felt it in his gut. She certainly hadn't gone out of her way to charm him. There was that awkward kiss she'd initiated. It proved to him that she wasn't as experienced as he'd thought. And he simply didn't care to deny himself anymore. These couple of weeks with Jane made him see that he was tired of being alone. It was time to take a chance.

There were several cars parked in front of the castle and he pulled in behind them. After shutting off the ignition he looked at Jane. "Looks like Mother has company."

"Yes." She caught the corner of her lip between her teeth.

J.P. got out of the car, then went around to the passenger side. She'd already opened her door, and he put his hands at her waist to help her down. Her skirt slid up her thigh and his palms ached to know the shape and texture of her skin.

Against the odds and with his eyes wide open, he realized he could be falling for a woman he only knew as Jane Doe.

He set her on her feet, but left his hands right where they were. His thumbs were millimeters from her breasts. The car's interior light illuminated the pounding pulse at the base of her slender throat. And that was a real and honest reaction to his nearness. He'd stake his entire fortune on it.

"Jane, if you're upset because I kissed you in my office, I—"

She shook her head. "Something happened that upset me. But it most definitely wasn't that kiss."

"Good. Because I intend to do it again."

"Wait, J.P. Before you do, there's something I have to tell you."

"I don't want to talk." He backed her up against the side of the car. "This is no time for conversation."

"But—"

He lowered his head and touched his lips to hers. Her resistance evaporated at the first contact. When her arms encircled his neck, he crushed her to him, savoring the softness of her breasts against his chest.

He wanted her like he'd never wanted another woman—in his bed and in his life. He didn't understand it. But with her in his arms, he couldn't find the will to care. He was as close to her as he could get without making love to her and he knew she could feel the evidence of his desire when a deep, sexy moan vibrated in her throat.

After several moments, she pulled her mouth from his. It was several heartbeats before she caught her breath enough to say, "J.P., we have to talk."

"Talking is highly overrated." It pleased him that her breathing was as unsteady as his own.

"I agree," she said with a frown. "But there's something you need to know."

"When I do, will you kiss me again?"

Lines of worry appeared between her eyes. "If you still want me to, there's nothing I'd like more."

He took her hand. "Then let's go inside."

They walked into the house. Voices drifted from the great room, and J.P. tugged her into the parlor. "Okay. Say it quick."

Jordan took a deep breath, partly to steady her breathing, partly to delay the inevitable. If he still wanted to kiss her after she told him the truth she would eat her very expensive mateless high heel.

She took her hand from his and stepped away from him. Feeling the warmth from his body simply made her want to melt into him again. And she wished she could, because when she told him who she was there was a good chance she'd never melt into him again. Just say it, she told herself.

"Okay. Here goes. I don't have amnesia."

There was the first bombshell. Now she had to say that her father, the man he disliked so intensely, had pushed her into the pretense she'd perpetrated. And that she'd assumed J.P. was an active participant in the whole thing.

Surely knowing her father the way he did, J.P. would be sympathetic. He would understand that she'd maintained the disguise to teach her father a lesson.

J.P. looked mildly surprised. "You got your memory back. That's why you were so quiet on the way back from the office. You should have said something. What's your name?"

"It's Jordan."

"At least we got the *J* part right. It's going to take a little time to stop thinking of you as 'Jane.' Jordan," he said, testing the name. "I like it. What's your last name?"

"It's Bish—"

But before she could finish, someone joined them in the parlor. Jordan's heart sank when she recognized the tall, blond, blue-eyed man.

Irritation at the interruption pulled J.P.'s mouth tight. "Who are you?"

"Clark Caldwell," he said, holding out his hand. "And if it isn't Jordan Bishop."

"Bishop?" J.P. stared at her.

Jordan saw shock, betrayal, anger and withdrawal cross his face. She recognized every last one because only a few hours ago in his office she'd felt them all when she realized he wasn't the hero in her father's plot.

"Yes," she confirmed.

"Harman Bishop's daughter?" he clarified.

"Unfortunately."

"You had us worried," Clark said. "Your father and I had no idea where you were."

"What are you doing here, Clark?" she demanded.

"Your father called me. He arrived just before I did. My estate is several miles from here."

She'd never been to Clark's place, and he'd never been to hers. Their relationship had never progressed that far. Suddenly all the pieces fell into place.

She looked at J.P. and assumed he was still in the same room with her only because he was still in shock. She had to make him understand. Later she would deal with why that was so very important.

"J.P., I was kidnapped. That was real."

"Oh?"

She winced at the bite of that one, short word.

"Yes. I had lunch with my father that day and someone grabbed me outside his office. I was scared to death. Then when the kidnapper did nothing but drive around, I calmed down and was able to think more rationally. I got away from him, just like I told you."

"Right."

This wasn't going well at all. She glared at Clark, wishing he would jump in and stick up for her. He could at least give her a character reference. Better yet, he could confirm the plot and his role in it.

"The kidnapper finally told me that my father was behind the whole thing. He'd set it up. Someone was supposed to rescue me. My 'hero,' the little weasel said. So when you came along right after he'd driven off, I thought you were in on the whole thing."

"And the point of this plot would be—what?" he asked, as he slid his hands into his pockets.

"I was supposed to fall in love with my rescuer," she said.

The derision in his expression caused her cheeks to burn. This story sounded completely ridiculous. But he knew her father. He knew what the man was capable of.

J.P.'s eyes hardened more if possible. "You expect me to believe your father plotted to kidnap his own daughter just to set her up with a guy?"

"It's true."

"This is Barbie and the baby all over again."

"I swear I'm telling the truth."

"Even if I believed you were kidnapped, why didn't you say anything to the sheriff? Why amnesia? Why pretend you didn't remember anything?"

"Because I needed to teach my father a lesson he'd never forget. I was scared within an inch of my life.

When I found out he was responsible, I can't even tell you how angry I was. He's done things before, but this was the worst. He's completely out of control."

"And the amnesia would punish him…how?"

"I figured you were in on it with him. That implied a certain level of friendship, probably a business relationship. I was waiting for you to show your true colors."

"To hit on you?"

She nodded. "When you did, I planned to tell you I knew what was going on. You would be humiliated and the fallout would affect my father personally and professionally. At least I hoped."

"And just why is he so determined to set you up?" J.P. asked sarcastically. "We may be in a castle, but this is 2004. The last time I checked, arranged marriages went out with powdered wigs and chastity belts."

His tone made her wince. But she took the fact that he was listening and asking questions as a good sign.

"He had a health scare earlier in the year." Leap year to be exact. She shivered as she remembered her wish. It sure as heck didn't feel as if it was coming true. "He got this wild idea that he won't be around much longer and decided he needed to find me a husband. But it was all about business."

"How's that?"

"He was always more interested in his business than in me. We never had much of a relationship, especially after my mother died. He buried himself in his job even more. I made it a point *not* to go into his line of work. He was afraid that if he died, there wouldn't be anyone to take over. Everything he worked so hard for all his life was my inheritance. If

I married a businessman who would safeguard it, he could relax.''

"Hmm."

"J.P., I honestly thought you were a workaholic just like my father. But the longer I knew you, the more I began to have doubts. I couldn't reconcile the caring family man I'd come to know as the self-centered manipulator I believed you to be. But I was sure you were in on this scheme right up until that moment in your office when I found out just how much you dislike my father.''

"That much of what you just said is definitely true.''

Jordan had known it would be an uphill battle to convince him. Now that she was losing the battle, it was instantly clear to her how important he'd become. Her desperation grew in direct proportion.

She'd forgotten Clark was there, but noticed him lounging in the doorway listening. "Obviously, Clark is the one who was supposed to rescue me. My father always liked him and this was his way of throwing us together.''

"So why did you think I was in on it?" J.P. asked.

"Until tonight, I didn't know Clark lived nearby. When you came along and I found out you did, it was a natural assumption that you were a coconspirator.''

"A natural assumption in whose universe?''

"I know it's an outrageous story. But Clark can confirm what I'm saying." She looked at her ex-boyfriend. "Go ahead. Tell him.''

"Tell him what?''

"The truth. That my father talked you into this. That you were supposed to 'rescue' me so I would fall in love with you. But you were late, and J.P. came along first. And did the rescuing,'' she finished.

Clark cleared his throat. ''Were you injured in the kidnapping, Jordan? Did you hit your head? You're really starting to scare me.''

She blinked at him, shock coursing through her. He was lying. She should have expected that. Catching him in lies was one of the reasons she'd broken off with him. ''You snake. I'm not sure what you hope to gain by this act, but I guarantee it's going to bite you in the backside.''

The jerk had the audacity to walk over to her and solicitously take her arm. ''Why don't you let me take you home?''

''Why don't you go straight to hell?'' she answered, yanking her arm from his grasp. ''I wouldn't go anywhere with you.''

''You don't mean that.'' His smile was condescending.

''I've never meant anything more. If you don't tell J.P. the truth, I'll call the sheriff and file charges against you for conspiracy to commit a kidnapping.''

''You can't prove anything,'' he said. ''And the reason you can't is because it isn't true.''

''Whether I can or not, the sheriff can make your life pretty darn miserable for a significant amount of time.''

She met J.P.'s hostile gaze and knew nothing she could do would bring her any satisfaction for what Clark's treachery had cost her.

Clark sighed. ''Maybe I'd better go, Jordan. Obviously Harman was wrong and my presence has upset you. I'll give you a call in a few days.''

''Don't waste your time.'' She blew out a long

breath. "For the record, Clark, you'll never get control of my father's company. Not ever. In case you were wondering."

Without another word, Clark left and J.P. was alone with Jordan. Apparently, he'd been stupid again. He'd needed a refresher course in the reality that trusting a woman was bad for his emotional health. Luckily for him, Jordan had shown him the error of his ways just in the nick of time.

"How long have you and your father been planning this little operation?" he asked.

"I haven't planned anything with my father. The only person who did just walked out of here."

He studied her, standing there with her hands on her curvy hips, looking indignant and innocent. Downright mad. She was good, he'd give her that. When life messed up the best-laid plans, by God, stand your ground and bluff with the big boys. She was looking quite the injured party as she met his gaze with her chin slightly lifted in defiance.

"It's not a secret to you that I think your father is manipulative."

"Yeah. I figured that out. And I've been trying to tell you, no one knows that better than I do. After this stunt—"

"Enough," he said, holding up his hand. "I don't believe a word that comes out of your mouth. There was a stunt pulled all right, and you were part of it."

"You arrogant bastard." Her eyes blazed. "And just what part do you think I played?"

"The one where you use your feminine attributes."

"I didn't use anything," she said with conviction. "You need to take responsibility for your own actions."

"What about when you kissed me?" he reminded her.

She blinked as a rosy color flooded her cheeks. "Okay. I forgot about that one."

He'd like to forget it, too. "For the record, the awkward, innocent, inexperienced act was really a nice touch."

"It wasn't an act." She looked at the floor for a moment, then back at him. "I'm not used to making the first move. Men come on to *me*. Like you, I always wonder whether it's about the family money."

He laughed, but there was no humor in it. "Isn't it rich that this time I've been duped, and it had nothing to do with wanting my money."

"I don't need it."

"You're an heiress in your own right. But I'd lay odds that you need your father's approval and would do anything for it. Including getting close to me to seal your father's deal."

"That's not how it was. I told you the truth about why I pretended amnesia. I was desperate to find a way to stop him. Not to mention angry as hell. I admit I lied. But I thought it was for a good reason."

"I don't think there's ever a good reason."

She tipped her head as she studied him. "Does self-righteousness keep you warm at night?"

"What's that supposed to mean?"

"It means you're an arrogant jackass to stand there and judge me. Is everything black and white with you?"

He ran his fingers through his hair. "You lied to my mother. My whole family. That makes it pretty black and white."

She caught her lip between her teeth. "I feel terrible

about that. But I felt so violated by what had happened to me, and I thought you were party to it.''

''My mother took you under her wing and worried about you. Did you get a laugh out of that?''

''Of course not. I plan to explain everything to her and apologize. I only hope she'll accept it.''

''She won't. Not if I have anything to say about it.''

She jerked as if he'd struck her. ''And you call me a manipulator.'' She sighed. ''I know my father's here somewhere. I saw his car out front. I'm going to make him tell you and Audrey what he did.''

''So you're going to stick with this absurd story?''

''A person can't go wrong sticking with the truth.''

''You're Harman Bishop's daughter. You wouldn't know the truth if it came up and shook your hand.''

J.P. saw her flinch again as she absorbed his meaning. It seemed to suck the bravado right out of her.

She blinked several times and took a deep breath. ''I wonder, J.P., if you're angry because I pretended to have amnesia, furious because I'm Harman Bishop's daughter or mad as hell because you were beginning to care for me?''

All of the above, he thought. But he wouldn't give her the satisfaction of a response. ''I think it's time for you to leave.''

She stared at him for several moments. ''I just have one more thing to say. I want you to know I'm sorry for what I did. I'll tell your mother the same thing. Send me a bill for all the expenses you incurred on my behalf.''

''I'll make sure your father gets it—''

''No,'' she said sharply. ''I'm responsible for myself. I'll call your secretary and give her my billing address. Tell my father I'll wait for him in the car.''

Head held high, Jordan walked past him. He hated that he felt even a glimmer of respect for the spirit and dignity she showed under the circumstances. He hated even more how empty he felt without her. He should be glad the deceitful witch was gone.

In his mind he listed her sins to fan the flames of his anger. With luck, he could burn away any lingering feelings for her.

But so far, luck hadn't been his friend.

Chapter Ten

Three weeks after the fiasco with J.P., Jordan looked across the restaurant table at her father and wondered what she was doing there. After leaving J.P., her father had taken her home and she'd given him a tongue-lashing that should have left scars on his ears and made her feel better. It hadn't. She'd never intended to speak to him again.

But Harman Bishop could be charming when he wanted. He'd coaxed her into this outing to make up for his meddling. He hadn't had to coax too hard because, truthfully, she'd yearned for a close relationship with him all her life. J.P. had been dead-on about her need for her father's approval. But he'd been dead wrong about how far she would go to get it.

She'd been down in the dumps ever since she'd walked out of the castle. Against the odds, she was hoping doing lunch with the man who was at least partially responsible for her bad mood could lift her spirits.

"I thought this place was your favorite," her father said, studying her intently.

She glanced around at the high ceilings, wood-panelled walls, cherry-wood furniture, crystal sconces and chandeliers that gave La Vie En Rose the ambience of a manor house. Fresh flowers and crisp white linen graced flat surfaces throughout the establishment.

"It is my favorite," she confirmed.

"I thought so. They serve entrees with asparagus spears standing at attention around a pork chop garnished with weeds, charge an arm and a leg for it and you leave the place hungry."

Absently, she moved her fork through the half-eaten food on her plate. "Hmm."

"Jordan, you've got to snap out of this."

She met her father's gaze over the lighted candle in the center of the table. It struck her that he was still a handsome man. His dark hair was streaked with gray—salt and pepper. It gave him a seasoned look, she thought, nearly smiling at her pun. His face with all its angles and hard lines could have been carved on Mount Rushmore. But it was lean and very nice looking. After his heart attack, he'd adopted a regimen of exercise and nutrition that improved his overall look as well as his long-term health.

"I don't have to snap out of anything," she said. "I'm entitled to be mad at you for as long as I want. This obscenely expensive restaurant is part of your penance."

"That's the spirit, honey." He reached across the table and covered her hand with his own. "What else can I do to make everything up to you?"

"Unless you can give J. P. Patterson selective amnesia—nothing."

"Here's the thing, Jordan." He cleared his throat. "I'll take responsibility for hiring the kidnapper and getting Clark on board to rescue you. But—"

"Speaking of bad rubbish, why in the world did he agree to be involved in this farce? It was about the company, wasn't it?"

"He loves you." When she stared at him without dignifying his explanation with a response, he threw up his hands in surrender. "Okay. You're right. I promised him the company," he said, confirming the guess she'd made that night.

"Good grief, Dad, what were you thinking?"

He squeezed her hand, then pulled his own back across the table. "I was thinking that Clark Caldwell is a good businessman who can successfully run the business when I'm not around anymore."

"So it's all about the company?"

"Of course not. It's about making sure you're taken care of."

Astonished, she stared at him. "And you expected that from Clark?"

"I know now that he's an opportunistic weasel. He tried to tell me you two were together when you first went missing. But he's a liar and not even very good at it. I saw through him pretty fast."

"But you called him after I called you. I know this because he showed up at the castle that night."

Harman ran his index finger through the condensation on his water glass. "I called to tell him there was no way he'd ever get his hands on my company. He arrived just before you and J.P., to try and change my mind."

Jordan remembered the way Clark had hung her out to dry that night and figured it was his way of getting even. "It just proves I was right about him. I broke it off because I'd rather go naked in a hailstorm than be with him."

"That's easy for you to say."

"No, it's not."

She knew her father hadn't meant it as a joke when his expression turned dark and the lines on either side of his nose and mouth grew deeper. "You didn't grow up poor or have to scratch out a living. You didn't wonder how to put food on the table or clothes on your child's back and a roof over her head. Your first memories are of a comfortable home with plenty of everything."

She'd never seen this pensive side of her father before. "Is that the way you grew up?"

"Yes. I remember the desperate look on my mother's face when I showed her a pair of shoes with holes in the soles and she didn't have any idea where she was going to get the money to buy me another pair. I swore that would never happen to my family."

"Dad, you never said anything."

"I didn't want to remember. I didn't want anything to cloud your perfect world."

"I didn't want perfect. I just wanted my father. But it explains a lot," she said. "Like why you were never home. Why you missed birthdays, anniversaries, recitals, school functions when I was growing up."

He shrugged. "It took me a lot of years to see that life is a trade-off. I could have success in business, but it would cost me time with my family. I'm sorry, Jordan. I wish I could say I didn't realize what was happening, but I did. It's just that I despised poverty. I love you more than my life. And I couldn't stand by and watch that happen to you."

Jordan cleared her throat of the emotion gathered there. "Speaking of shoes, when your lackey grabbed me from my office, I lost a very expensive one."

She remembered J.P. had sarcastically asked if she'd lost her glass slipper. She'd responded with a taunting question of her own about him being the prince. She'd had no idea he truly was—so to speak.

The corners of her father's mouth turned up. "I'll buy you another pricey pair."

"I'll let you."

If only he could buy her another life. But it was up to her to make the best of this one. Making peace and having a relationship with him would help.

"Okay, Dad, so now I know what you were thinking. But you have to admit the kidnapping was over-the-top. The worst part is that I like J.P. a lot and he'll never speak to me again."

"I'll admit it was over the top. But you have to take responsibility for some of the mess. You came up with the amnesia angle all by yourself."

"That was to get even with you. I needed to make a major statement and going quietly wouldn't do it."

He grinned suddenly. "You're your father's daughter after all."

Probably, she thought. "It seemed like a good idea at the time. The problem was, the longer I knew J.P., the more I liked him. And I couldn't figure out how that could happen with a guy you picked out for me."

"I'd take exception to that, but the guy I picked out is a loser. If only he'd been punctual—"

She huffed out a breath. "Dad, he's smarmy. Even if he'd shown up, I don't like him. I never liked him. I never will like him. He refused to corroborate my story and own up to his part in the whole thing."

At least her father had confessed to Audrey that night. But when he'd tried to reason with her son, J.P. had walked out, refusing to listen. Should she take it as a hopeful sign that J.P. had let her explain? Probably not, since she hadn't heard a word from him since.

"You were right to dump Clark. I should have trusted your judgment." He held up his hand, palm out. "I'll never meddle in your love life again."

She snorted. "Like I believe that."

He fiddled with his water glass. "I won't have time, since I'll be busy with my own life."

"You've got a love life?" she said.

He met her gaze. "Don't sound so surprised. I'm not such a bad-looking guy."

"It's not that. I just—"

"Didn't think an old guy like me had it in him?"

"I didn't think you'd make time for a relationship," she admitted.

"It found me," he said. "I told you Audrey and I knew each other years ago. We had a falling out— some silly misunderstanding that I can't even remember now. I think I wasn't ready to settle down. When I was, I met your mother and we fell in love."

"I still miss her," Jordan said.

"Me, too." He met her gaze and the sadness in his own was obvious. "But I've been lonely. Seeing Audrey again made me realize how much. And I've seen her every night since picking you up at the castle."

Her eyes widened. "You have?"

He nodded. "I explained everything to her, about my part in the plot. She gave me quite an earful about that."

"Good for her. I knew I liked her."

"Do you really?"

"Very much," Jordan confirmed. "For all the good that does me now."

"She doesn't hold a grudge. In fact she thinks you're quite inventive and spirited. She admires the way you can think on your feet."

"I guess that's something."

"But she's worried about J.P. She can't convince him to lighten up about the incident. She thinks he cares about you a lot."

"She's wrong."

"He'd be a fool not to care. You're beautiful, smart and have a pretty good sense of humor when you're not mad at your old man."

Jordan picked up the butter knife and stabbed the little balls in the iced dish. "He's had some unfortunate experiences. Women are after his money. One of them was pregnant and said the baby was his. He was going to marry her. It hit him hard when the truth came out."

"That's another thing you've got going for you. You don't need his money. And you're not pregnant. Are you?" he asked, eyes narrowing.

"Of course not."

Although she almost wished she was. She'd love to have a baby, and J.P. would be a fabulous father. But how like her own father to miss the point. He was making progress, but he needed some serious practice in flexing his emotional muscles.

"J.P. thinks you put me up to faking amnesia to somehow facilitate the merger between the two companies."

"That doesn't make any sense."

"It does to him. Because of his past. And the fact

is, I lied to him. I'm just one more in a long line of women who used him. Just because I'm not a gold digger doesn't mean I'm any different or that he'll ever forgive me.''

Her father put his hand over hers to stop the butter massacre. "Give him some time, Jordan. He'll see that he's wrong about you."

"I'm not holding my breath." And it was too painful to talk about. Time to change the subject. "But tell me more about you and Audrey."

"I'm going to do everything I can to make it work with her. Funny how a brush with death sends a message, loud and clear, that life is too short to waste. When you know something is right, you have to go for it."

Jordan blinked in surprise. "Are you saying you're going to ask her to marry you?"

He met her gaze and there was stubborn determination in his. "When I'm sure of getting a yes."

"I'm glad, Dad. I think Audrey's been lonely, too. I'd like to see her find happiness."

"It's my plan to make her happy." He moved the knife out of her reach. "Now about you and J.P."

"There is no me and J.P." She shook her head. "But at least you'll be happy. That should take some of the sting out of the fact that I'm more miserable than I've ever been in my entire life."

"Come on, Jordan. You're a Bishop. Stiff upper lip and all that. Besides, he doesn't mean what he says."

She glanced up quickly. "He doesn't? Do you know something? What did he say?"

"I don't know anything. That's not what I meant." Her father shifted in his chair and wouldn't meet her gaze.

"Come on, Dad. Spill it. What do you know?"

"According to Audrey, he says he'll never forgive you. But he doesn't mean that. Besides, never is a long time."

"Yes, it is," she said, her voice unsteady, her lips quivering. She had a bad feeling J.P. could out-stubborn even her father. "Thanks for this cheering up lunch, Dad. It helped a lot."

Then she burst into tears.

J.P. sat in his office staring at the computer screen. He'd been trying to catch up on his e-mail, but kept reading the same message over and over, then couldn't remember what it said. Instead of the words, he kept seeing a pair of very dark, very beautiful eyes filled with disillusionment, anger and sadness. How could she distract him even now? It had been three weeks. She'd played him for a fool; he knew better than to give her another opportunity.

No matter how empty his life felt without her in it.

On top of being humiliated, he missed Jane—Jordan. At least the *J* part was right. She'd worked her way inside him with her sharp wit and sassy come-backs. How ironic that the woman who finally caught his attention was after her father's deal. Her motivation was money, just not his. That should have made it impersonal.

But it felt very personal, and he hated that.

Suddenly, his office door slammed open and Harman Bishop was standing there. He had the nerve to be glaring. "You son of a—"

The intercom buzzed and J.P. pushed the button. "Mr. Patterson, Mr. Bishop is here to see you. But I guess you already know. Sorry, sir, I couldn't stop him.''

''It's all right, Dolores.''

''Do you want me to call security?''

''No. I'll take care of this.''

J.P. switched off then stood and walked around his desk to face the man. ''Get out of my office.''

''Not until I do what I came here to do.''

''And what would that be?''

Harman Bishop walked across the room and stopped a foot away. ''I'm here to take you apart.''

J.P. wanted to laugh. It was on the tip of his tongue to say ''you and what army.'' Although the old guy looked pretty fit, it still wouldn't be a fair fight. ''And why would you want to do that?''

''For starters, you made Jordan cry.''

''I did? I haven't seen her for weeks.'' He left his arms at his sides, ready to defend himself, watching the other man's every move.

''You arrogant little pip-squeak—'' Bishop curled his fingers into a fist, resting his thumb over them. He'd been in a battle or two, J.P. thought. His own father had taught him that if he was ever serious about hitting someone, never tuck his thumb inside or he'd break it.

''No one makes my little girl cry and gets away with it.''

''Look, Bishop, my father taught me not to start a fight, but if it happens—finish it. And it would give me great pleasure to beat the crap out of you.''

Harman's eyes narrowed. ''Let's go. What are you waiting for?''

''My mother advised me to use words instead of my fists.'' Something flickered in the other man's gaze at the mention of J.P.'s mother. "Let's be honest. *If* Jordan is unhappy, it's not because of anything I did."

They were practically nose to nose and J.P. knew when the other man blinked. Letting out a long breath, he uncurled his fingers.

"You're right," Harman said, a gleam stealing into his eyes. "Jordan is unhappy and it's her own fault."

J.P. narrowed his gaze on the other man. "Is this another manipulation?"

"Like you said. Let's be honest. It's nothing more than like father, like daughter." Bishop shrugged.

J.P. rejected that with every fiber of his being. Jordan was nothing like her father. "Mother said you confessed your part in this scheme."

He nodded. "I planned everything. Including bullying her into having lunch with me that day so the guy would know where to grab her."

"Right." He thought about the hero portion of the program, and his gut knotted when he remembered Jordan's boyfriend. "Where did Caldwell fit in?"

"Clark was in on the planning stage," he admitted. "I like Clark. He has potential."

"For what? Most likely to succeed in prison?"

"A head for business and potential for Jordan's personal life." Bishop ran his fingers through his hair. "He said he cared about her and was convinced she would change her mind about him if she saw him as her hero."

"You're telling me he came up with this stupid idea?"

"I'm not going to lie to you, Patterson. I don't know who came up with it first. It sort of evolved over drinks when we were brainstorming. But I take full responsibility."

"I don't understand how you could sanction something like this."

He shook his head. "I've been asking myself that. I went a little off the deep end, I guess. In February, the twenty-ninth as a matter of fact, Jordan's birthday—"

"Leap year?"

He nodded. "I had a mild heart attack. Something like that makes a man stop and think. It hit me that I wouldn't be around forever to take care of her. And I haven't been a very good father. I've neglected my daughter for twenty-four years. Lately, I guess I've been trying to make it up to her. I sort of went over the top."

"You think?" J.P. said sarcastically.

The older man glared. "If something happens to me, I need to make sure Jordan is taken care of."

"By Clark Caldwell?" J.P. couldn't keep the derision out of his tone.

"That's what Jordan said. But she'll come around."

Everything in J.P. rebelled at the thought. "Stay out of her life, Bishop."

"You spoiled, snot-nosed kid. You've had everything handed to you on a silver platter." He rested his hands on his hips as his gaze narrowed. "I built a multimillion-dollar company with my bare hands. I want to make sure there's someone at the helm who will protect what I built."

The thought of Jordan with a creep Bishop had picked for her tied J.P.'s gut in knots. To the list of all the other feelings he didn't understand, he added jealousy. "Again I have to say—Clark Caldwell?"

"I don't see anyone else around who's qualified and willing to put up with Jordan."

Put up with her? A guy would be lucky to have her in his life. "So it's all true." He finally acknowledged to himself that she'd been an innocent victim. "You really did set up the whole thing to find her a husband and someone to take over the company?"

"Yeah. But she came up with the fake amnesia bit all by herself. It never would have occurred to me. I have to admire her resourcefulness—even if it is underhanded."

J.P. regretted that he'd been brought up not to start a fight. This guy was a piece of work. No wonder Jordan had snapped. "There's nothing underhanded about her. She's strong and spirited and smart. She was just fighting back the best way she knew how."

"If you say so. But I've tried to put myself in her shoes...." He shrugged.

J.P. remembered her on that lonely stretch of road on the way to his estate. She was walking in a circle with one high heel missing—disheveled, torn nylons, traces of fear in her eyes. How would he have felt in that situation? Pretty damn furious.

Bishop shook his head. "Deception is never okay. She thought punishing me was a good excuse. She figured it would stop me from trying to find her a man. But her scheme backfired. Because she fell in love with the man, in spite of the fact that she thought I picked him out. That's rich, isn't it? Because you're probably the last guy on the planet I would pick for my little girl."

Love? J.P. ran his fingers through his hair. "I don't know what to say to that."

"I don't want to hear anything from you. All you have to do is listen. I just came from lunch with her and promised I wouldn't interfere ever again—"

"You mean like now?"

One corner of his mouth turned up. "This is the last time."

"What does that mean?"

He sighed. "Do you mind if we sit?"

"Suit yourself." J.P. rounded his desk and took a position of power in his chair.

Bishop lowered himself into one of the tufted leather wing-back chairs. "I've loved two women in my life. The first one was Jordan's mother. I worked hard, long hours. But I told myself it would pay off and we'd have years together to enjoy the rewards of my work. But she died way too young, and I buried myself in work because I couldn't face the fact that I wouldn't grow old with her."

"Who's the other woman?"

"Audrey Patterson."

J.P. was shocked. He'd known his mother was involved with someone. And she was happier than he'd seen her since his father had passed. But she'd refused to tell him who the man was. Now he knew why. "Mother and I need to have a talk."

Bishop nodded. "Figured you would. But we knew each other a long time ago. I never forgot her. Your mother is a wonderful woman."

"Too good for you."

The words were automatic. J.P. wasn't so sure he meant them. After all, his mother had impeccable judgment. She could spot the character in a person— good or bad. And she liked Jordan. He'd deliberately overlooked that fact because he didn't want Audrey to be right. Then he would have to take a chance. And this time being wrong would be so much worse.

"Probably," Bishop acknowledged. "But I'm not

going to question my good fortune. And neither should you.''

''What's that supposed to mean?''

''Jordan is a wonderful woman, too. And here's another unsolicited piece of advice—you're too good for her.''

''What makes you think I'm interested?'' he bluffed.

''Audrey says so.''

J.P. knew his mother had exhibited impeccable instincts time and time again. So he had to trust that she knew what she was doing with Harman Bishop. And Jordan... He hadn't been able to get her out of his mind. He remembered what Bishop had said when he'd first walked in. Jordan had cried—over him. ''How is Jordan?''

The other man frowned, then shrugged. ''She's coming around. She'll get over you.''

Would she? Did he want her to? J.P. had been miserable, too, and figured he was going to hell for being so happy Jordan was feeling the same way.

''That's all I have to say.'' The other man stood and walked to the door. ''On second thought, there's one more thing.''

''Okay.''

''It would be in your best interest to forget about Jordan. You're all wrong for her.''

''According to you, my mother disagrees.''

''Audrey's too close to the situation to be objective,'' he said, his eyes narrowing. ''I advise you to stay away from my daughter.''

''And why should I?''

He smiled, but there was no warmth in it. ''Because if you hurt her any more, I'll spend the rest of the days

God grants me on this earth working to make you sorry instead of working to make your mother happy.''

The best comeback he could manage was, ''Is that so?''

''Count on it.'' Bishop opened the door and said, ''Have a nice day.'' Then he was gone.

J.P. hadn't had a peaceful day since he'd caught Jordan in his arms on that deserted road. And he hadn't had a nice day since she'd walked out of his house. If he was honest, he had to admit he'd never felt like this about any woman.

But what the hell had just happened? He rubbed the back of his neck as he leaned back in his chair, replaying in his mind the things Harman Bishop had said. Suddenly the ''aha'' light went on. That sly old fox had gotten J.P. to defend her. No wonder his corporation was so successful. If her old man had come in here glorifying Jordan's virtues, J.P. would have dug in his heels and resisted. Instead, he'd trashed her, getting J.P. to defend her. In the process, J.P. had realized something very important.

He couldn't shut his feelings down anymore. He couldn't stop the flood of emotions. It was official. He was in love with Jordan Bishop.

Chapter Eleven

Jordan looked around the luxury condominium complex. It was quiet and lushly landscaped with rows of yellow, pink, purple and fuchsia flowers everywhere. The condo unit she wanted was right in front of her and staring at Mother Nature in all her glory was simply procrastinating. It was time to get this over with.

Taking a deep breath, she knocked on the door and waited, heart pounding. She heard footsteps from inside and guessed the entryway floor was wood. That's what she would have expected. Warm and inviting, like the condo's owner.

Then Audrey Patterson opened the door and smiled with genuine pleasure. "Jane. I mean Jordan. It's going to take some time to get used to your real name."

Time was something Jordan knew she didn't deserve from this woman. "May I come in, Mrs. Patterson?"

"Of course, dear." She stepped back and opened

the door wider. After shutting it, she said, "Can I get you a cold drink? Or some tea and cookies, perhaps?"

"Please don't be nice to me," Jordan blurted out.

"But why not?" Blue eyes, wide, kind and innocent stared into her own. "Please come in and make yourself comfortable. We need to talk."

She led Jordan into a large living room furnished with an overstuffed white corner group and oak occasional tables. Colorful throw pillows scattered over the sofa added texture and personality. The room was sophisticated and expensively furnished at the same time it oozed warmth and charm. Just like Audrey.

While the other woman made tea, Jordan did as she was told and perched on the short side of the cushy sofa. She sat, but just on the edge, not making herself comfortable even though she'd been invited to do just that. And this particular piece of furniture practically begged a body to burrow in and be cozy.

"Here you are, dear," Audrey said, handing her a china teacup on a matching saucer.

"Thank you. I appreciate your kindness even though I don't deserve it."

Audrey sat on the other sofa beside her. Their knees would have bumped if Jordan had been taller. "Now tell me why you think I should be angry with you."

"Because I deceived you." She took a sip of tea, hoping it would calm her nervous stomach. "I know J.P. has talked to you and so has my father."

She nodded. "Harm told me why you felt compelled to make a point after what he'd done."

"I waited until your renovations were complete and you moved back here before coming to apologize for my abominable behavior." She took a deep breath. "In my own defense, let me just say that being kidnapped was the straw that broke the camel's back. I'd been frightened and traumatized. I'm not a liar. Apparently, I just snapped. I didn't mean to hurt anyone.''

''With the possible exception of your father.''

Jordan nodded. ''And J.P. At first. As soon as I found out he wasn't involved, I planned to tell him the truth.''

''But things spun out of control before you had the opportunity.''

''Yes. Mrs. Patterson—''

''You used to call me Audrey.'' She smiled kindly. ''There's no reason why you shouldn't still.''

Jordan took comfort from that. This woman had never been anything but gracious and good-hearted. But she'd been played false and her son had been hurt. What mother could get over that?

''Audrey, I just came here to say that I'm very sorry for not telling you the truth. I hope someday you can find a way to forgive me for what I did to you.''

''For providing the most entertainment I've had in a very long time? Good gracious, Jordan, there's nothing to forgive.''

Jordan blinked at her. ''Really?''

''I knew practically from the beginning that you were faking it.''

Well, that was stunning. ''You did? How?''

''Instinct.'' She smiled serenely. ''And on all the soap operas and numerous romance novels it frequently happens that way. I believed you'd been through a trauma. But I was fairly certain you knew who you were.''

''But you took me in. You gave me safe harbor. You insisted the sheriff not take me back to town. You could have had him lock me up and throw away the key. Why didn't you?''

''I wanted to see what you were up to.'' Her eyes were twinkling with mischief. ''And I saw the way my son was looking at you.''

''As if he'd like to strangle me.''

She shook her head. ''As if he'd like to seduce you.''

Shocked didn't begin to describe what Jordan was feeling. She shook her head. ''Are we talking about the same J. P. Patterson? The day he found me on the road? Missing a shoe? My panty hose in tatters?''

''Yes, indeed.''

''No offense, but you must be mistaken.''

''I know my son, Jordan. He was taken with you from the beginning. Cautious and concerned because of his past to be sure, but you definitely had his attention. And therein lies his conflict. How could he be smitten with a woman he didn't trust, who is the daughter of the man he's engaged in rigorous business negotiations with.''

''Yeah.'' Way to make me feel better, she wanted to say. But cheaters never prosper and she'd cheated this woman. ''He might have been able to get over the deception if my father was anyone but Harman Bishop.''

''You say that as if it's a bad thing.''

''Isn't it?'' Jordan watched myriad expressions pass over the other woman's face. Did she share her father's deep and tender feelings?

''Harman is not perfect.''

''You can say that again,'' Jordan said wryly.

''His methods might be questionable. No editorializing,'' she said, pointing a finger. ''But his heart is in the right place. You don't find it incredibly dear and romantic that he went to all the trouble of setting up a scenario for you to fall in love?''

And it had worked. Just not with the man her father had intended. But she couldn't say that to the mother of the man she'd fallen for. The woman her father was in love with.

"I'll concede that my father means well. But he can't go around tampering with my life anymore.''

Audrey patted her hand. "He won't. I guarantee it.''

"How can you do that?''

"For one thing, he can see how much this has hurt you. He feels horrible about that. He's truly sorry for what he's done.''

"I know.'' Jordan believed that or she wouldn't have opened up to him the way she had over lunch. But how ironic that in his zeal to find her a husband, he'd actually cost her the one man who could make her happy.

Audrey let out a long breath. "And I can promise you he's going to have other things to think about besides you. I intend to keep him very busy.''

Jordan smiled. "So you're going to give him a yes when he asks you to marry him?''

"I'll keep him on his toes a bit longer, but if he proposes, I plan to say yes.''

"That's wonderful.''

"Is it?'' Audrey's expression turned pensive. "Are you truly happy about us? I wouldn't presume to be a stepmother at this stage of the game. But I hope we can be friends.''

"There's nothing I'd like more,'' Jordan said sincerely. "Actually, that's not true.''

"It's not?''

She shook her head. "In spite of what I did, I'm a very honest person. So please believe me when I tell you that while I was deceiving you, while you took me in no questions asked, you made me miss my mother less than I have in a very long time."

"That's a lovely thing to say, dear."

"And I mean it sincerely. I'll look forward to having a relationship with you—friend, stepmother, whatever you want it to be."

"Thank you, Jordan."

"Does J.P. know yet?"

"He knows I'm seeing your father and he's being terribly snarky about it."

Jordan wanted to smile at her word choice. Then she remembered that J.P. hated both of the Bishops. "Audrey, be careful. I love the idea of you and Dad together. But J.P. is important to you. What if—"

"He'll come around."

"What if he doesn't?"

"He will. You'll see."

"How can you be so sure?"

"Because he loves you, dear."

Her gaze snapped to the other woman's so fast, Jordan feared whiplash. "What?"

"I said he loves you."

"You're wrong."

"Tsk tsk," Audrey said, waggling her finger. "That's not the way to win the approval of your future wicked stepmother."

"Sorry. I didn't mean it to come out so harshly. But I can't see how that could be. He didn't trust me from the beginning. Then he found out that my father is his business rival. There's no way he'll ever trust me, let alone care about me."

"You're wrong."

Jordan couldn't help a small smile. "Now who's not winning approval."

"I'm old. I can say anything I want without worrying about the fallout." She grinned wickedly, but the look faded quickly. "J.P. had a chance to see your inner beauty. Your willingness to pitch in with family. Your interaction with Val and the other children at her party. You can fool people some of the time. But you can't fool children—ever. Val adores you."

"That's something," Jordan said with a sigh.

"How do you feel about my son?"

Jordan looked down at the teacup in her hands, resting in her lap. She put the delicate china on the table, then found herself twisting her fingers together. "I hardly know him," she hedged.

Audrey's warm blue-eyed gaze turned piercing. "Let me ask you this way. If *he* proposed, what would *you* say?"

Yes, was her instant thought. Out loud she said, "It's a pointless question and a waste of breath. He'll never get past what I did and who my father is. If I were the last woman on earth, he would never be able to love me."

"That answers my question. You're in love with him," Audrey said.

Jordan sighed. "It's important to me that you know I would never do anything to hurt him ever again."

Audrey studied her, then a satisfied smile turned up the corners of her mouth.

At least she'd made someone happy, Jordan thought.

Jordan was in her branch office of Elite Interiors, organizing her material swatches. She was grouping together the brushed cotton twills and the chenilles after clients had mixed them up while matching paint chips and wallpaper samples. Work was the best medicine for what ailed her. Busy hands are happy hands, her mother had always said. At least that part of her would be happy. Everything else was wretchedly miserable.

Including her heart. Especially her heart.

It was Friday night. Six o'clock, closing time. The evening loomed ahead of her but she refused to put the adjectives empty and lonely in front it. Her life was full. She would simply find something else to organize.

The shop door opened, and she was pathetically grateful. With luck, the customer would keep her here overtime. She didn't mind; she loved her job.

"May I help you with something," she said, turning toward the newcomer. When she saw who was there, she grinned. Her two very best friends. "Rach. Ash. Boy, am I glad to see you two."

"Hi, Jordan." Blond, blue-eyed Rachel Manning wove her way through fabric display racks and tables piled high with wallpaper books. She was the maternal one of the group and when she stopped, her arms opened wide for a hug.

Ashley Gallagher trailed right behind. She was a redhead with a personality to match, spirited and unpredictable. "Group hug," she said, joining in the greeting.

Ending the embrace, Jordan said, "What are you guys doing here? It's a long drive from Sweet Spring."

"Not that long," Rachel answered. "And we wanted

to surprise you. The three of us are in desperate need of a catch-up session.''

''I couldn't agree more,'' Jordan said. ''I know this great little cafe in the West End with terrific food and atmosphere.''

''It's Friday night and likely to be crowded and loud.'' Ashley tucked a strand of copper-colored hair behind her ear. ''We picked up Chinese and a bottle of wine so we don't have to go anywhere.''

Jordan nodded. ''Even better. I've got a small break room in the back. Just let me lock the front door and shut off the lights in the showroom.''

A short time later, they were settled around the small, circular table and everyone had a plate filled with their favorites—beef and broccoli, cashew chicken, chow mein and egg rolls and a full glass of chardonnay.

Jordan took a sip of wine, then set her glass down. ''So, tell me what's going on with you two. Rachel, how's Emma?''

Her friend smiled a soft, maternal smile filled with tenderness, the look she always wore when someone asked about her infant daughter. ''She's absolutely perfect. Jake and I are hoping the adoption will be finalized soon.''

''And how are you and Jake?'' Jordan asked.

She smiled again and her expression wasn't maternal, but still tender. There'd been a time when Rachel and Jake Fletcher were on opposite sides of a legal battle for custody of Emma. Against the odds, they'd fallen in love.

''Jake and I set a date for the wedding. It's right around Thanksgiving.''

''Very appropriate,'' Jordan said. She looked at

Ashley. "And what about you, missy? What's happening in your life?"

Her friend's brown eyes glowed. "Max and I are getting married, too."

Jordan put down her fork and took their hands. "I'm so happy for you guys."

"Now we want to know what's going on with you," Rachel said.

"You know." She shrugged. "Work. The usual."

Ashley's eyes narrowed. "There's been nothing 'usual' about us since our birthday in New Orleans when we made our wishes."

"She's right," Rachel said. "I asked for a baby and look what happened."

"I wished for money and power," Ashley chimed in. "Because of my promotion at Caine Chocolate Company, Max and I were reunited and fell in love."

Jordan looked from one to the other. "So what is it you're asking me?"

"Your wish," Rachel said, leaning forward with eager anticipation. "It was the most outrageous. Any sign of it coming true?"

"No."

One small word, one gigantic hurt. And so much more. It meant her chances of personal happiness were slim to none. She just knew, like she knew her friends loved and supported her, that J. P. Patterson was the man she'd always yearned for. Now he was the man she loved who would never love her back.

Jordan looked at the glowing faces of her friends and felt a twinge she knew was envy. She was part terrible person and part flawed human being. She was happy for her friends. She truly was. But their wishes had come true, bringing them love. It was probably all a coincidence. Otherwise her wish would have come true, too.

Unless she was being punished by the gods. She'd been so cavalier, challenging to the extreme. Good grief—a princess who lived in a palace. What had she been thinking?

Ashley took a sip of her wine. "So you're telling us that you haven't met a man?"

"Actually, I have."

"Is he a prince?" Rachel asked.

"Prince is his middle name," Jordan admitted.

"I didn't ask if he's a great guy. I want to know if he's royalty."

One corner of Jordan's mouth lifted. "He's not royalty. His middle name really is Prince. It's a family name on his mother's side."

"No," Rachel said, obviously surprised. Then she stared. "What is it, Jordy? There's something else, isn't there?"

"What makes you think that?"

Ashley waved her fork. "You've got that look on your face."

"What look?" she said.

"The one you get when you're hiding something. Something you don't want to talk about," Rachel added.

"What's his name?"

Jordan sighed. "Jonathan Prince Patterson. He goes by J.P."

Ashley frowned. "I've heard of him. Patterson, Inc. Before Max took over running the family chocolate company, when he was a freelance corporate consultant, he did business with J. P. Patterson."

"Really?" Small world, Jordan thought.

"Yes. And there's something about him that stuck in my mind, but I can't put my finger on it."

"Apparently, it didn't stick very well," Jordan said, grinning.

"Okay. You met a Prince, so to speak," Rachel pointed out. "The rest of your wish was to live in a palace."

"That's it," Ashley said, snapping her fingers. She shot a triumphant look at each of her friends. "Max told me the interesting thing is that J. P. Patterson lives in a castle, halfway between here and Sweet Spring."

"Is that true?" Rachel asked, clearly shocked.

Jordan nodded. "His family made their money in cattle during the late 1800s. They didn't know what to do with the cash and someone got the bright idea to buy a palace in England and move it here brick by brick and reassemble it."

"Sounds like someone had a lot of time on their hands," Rachel commented.

"It also sounds like your wish is two-thirds granted," Ashley pointed out.

"Aside from the obvious fact that I'm not a princess, there's a fatal flaw preventing my wish." Jordan struggled to keep her voice from betraying the sadness she felt.

"And what might that be?" her friends asked together.

"I'm not ever going to live in that castle."

She finally broke down and told them everything about her father arranging the kidnapping and her ill-fated decision to feign amnesia.

"He was pretty mad at me," she finished. "After what I did, he wouldn't rent me a room in his castle, let alone make me his princess."

"That's what you get for being the adventurous one, with the wild ideas," Rachel pointed out. "But you're also the one who doesn't understand the word no. It's not like you to give up so easily."

"If you want him," Ashley added. "I think you're wrong about not getting your wish, Jordan."

"And why is that?"

"Don't you see." Ashley leaned forward eagerly. "For Rach and me, our wishes set in motion a chain of events that brought us our heart's desire. Just like Faith the Gypsy said. And for the record, I'm beginning to believe she's the real McCoy."

Rachel nodded. "I see where you're going. She said one wish is all you need if it's the right one. And if we wished for our heart's desire, we'd be rewarded."

Rachel finished the wine in her glass. "But we all agreed not to wish for a man."

"So you guys just got lucky," Jordan said with a shrug.

"And so will you. If I were you, I'd get your dad an extra special something next Father's Day," Ashley said. "He started it with the kidnapping. But you were meant to wind up where J.P. could find you. It's magic."

"That's right." Rachel was practically vibrating with excitement. "Remember Faith said magic works in mysterious ways."

"And I believe I made fun of the whole experience." Jordan winced as memories of her sarcasm played through her mind. If only she could arrange selective amnesia. There were a lot of things between then and now she'd like to wipe from her memory.

"You were the one who saved the lamp," Rachel pointed out.

Jordan moved her food around her plate with her fork. "So it's a good news, bad news thing. I get two-thirds of my wish—seen the palace, met the guy who owns it. Unfortunately, through my fault and a little help from my father, the handsome prince has turned into a toad."

"It's not over till it's over," Rachel said.

Ashley looked at her and nodded. "I agree. I made the mistake of believing the worst about Max and was sure he would never forgive me. I've never been happier to be wrong."

"It's a good pep talk." Jordan reached out and took her friend's hands in hers. "I don't buy into it, but I feel better now. I was pretty bummed when you walked in tonight. I don't know how you knew I needed you, but I'm more grateful than I can say for your friendship. Thanks for cheering me up."

"Don't write J.P. off yet," Rachel advised.

Ashley squeezed her hand. "Don't rule out the magic factor."

Jordan swallowed the lump of emotion in her throat. In spite of their recently discovered happiness, she didn't believe in magic.

Chapter Twelve

J.P. stood by the stone fireplace in the waiting area of the Italian restaurant where his mother had asked him to meet her. Sisley's was written up in magazines and featured in newspapers as the premier romantic rendezvous spot in the area. One article had touted its ambience and the fact that more couples became engaged here than anywhere else in the state of Texas.

The hostess approached him. The woman was in her forties, blond, blue-eyed and dressed in a black, long-sleeved dress. Very elegant.

"Mr. Patterson," she said, her voice soft with a cultured Southern accent, "Are you certain you don't wish to be seated? When your mother phoned to say she would be late, she asked that you be shown to a table when you arrived."

"No, thanks. I'd like to escort her to the table. She hates to walk into a room alone."

That was a lie. Audrey didn't give a damn. But there was something going on. He could feel it. Other than the fact that this place catered to couples in love, he figured his mother would call him on his cell to let him know she was running late. Now he was curious.

"Very well. May I get you something from the bar?"

He shook his head. "I'll wait for her."

He pulled his cell phone from his jacket and hit the speed dial for his mother's number. When he got voice mail, he flipped the phone closed.

He looked at his watch and wondered what Audrey was up to. Several moments later, the restaurant door opened and Jordan Bishop walked in, answering the question. Then he forgot the question and the answer as his pulse rate hiked. Blood raced through his veins and pounded in his ears. She looked wonderful in a tan skirt that was just short enough to make a man yearn to slide his hand the rest of the way up her thigh. Her matching jacket hugged her slender waist and curvy hips. She looked good—a sight for very sore eyes.

She glanced around the crowded waiting area as if she were looking for someone, but didn't notice him in the shadowed corner. As she stopped in front of the hostess, he could see Jordan's profile even though her face was partially hidden by the dark, silk curtain of her hair. His fingers ached to touch it, to slide through the soft strands, cup her face in his palms.

"Hi," she said to the hostess. One corner of her mouth curved up. "I'm Jordan Bishop. My father made a reservation for two. Is he here yet?"

Things were suddenly crystal clear, J.P. thought. Definitely a setup.

The hostess looked down and checked her book.

"I have it right here, Miss Bishop. I'll have the maitre d' take you to your table."

"Thank you." She opened her purse and looked for something inside.

J.P. moved toward her and stopped. "Hello, Jordan."

The pulse at the base of her throat fluttered wildly. She looked up and stared at him, surprised. "What are you doing here?"

"It's a restaurant. I'm having dinner."

"What a coincidence. So am I." Her gaze narrowed. "Just so there's no misunderstanding, I had no idea you'd be here."

"The thought never crossed my mind."

"My father asked me to meet him here," she said defensively. Her chin lifted. "But maybe it would be better if I just leave now."

She turned and walked out the door before he could stop her. J.P. followed. He let her go once because he'd been too cynical to trust what his gut told him. He wasn't going to make the same mistake again.

"Jordan. Wait."

She kept walking, but fortunately her legs were short and she was wearing high heels. He easily caught up with her and took hold of her upper arm to stop her.

"Wait," he said again.

The outside of Sisley's was done in cobblestones and lush plants. Wrought-iron benches were scattered around the exterior for effect as well as for customers to sit and wait. At the moment he and Jordan were alone.

J.P. released her arm. "We need to talk."

"I had no idea you would be here. It's just an unfortunate coincidence that we ran into each other here.''

"Right. A coincidence. In the most romantic restaurant in town.''

"Look, J.P., I can't make you believe me, but—''

"I believe you.''

"You do?''

He nodded. "My mother asked me to meet her here.''

Jordan's eyes widened with comprehension. "Ah. There's mischief afoot.''

"Yeah. Mother called and insisted they seat me while I waited for her. Apparently she thought that would make it more difficult for me to leave when you came in.''

"But you didn't take a table.''

"No. I had a feeling something was up.''

"And you were right. Welcome to my world.''

"Yes.'' He slid his hands into his pockets. "I have a clue now about what you've been going through with your father.''

"Some of it is rubbing off on your mother.''

"Yeah,'' he said.

"We dodged a bullet on that one. Take care, J.P.''

As she turned away, he quickly reached out again and took her arm, sliding his fingers down to loosely hold her wrist. "Wait.''

The breeze blew her hair across her face and she brushed it back. "Why? We have nothing left to say to each other.''

That wasn't true. And holding her wrist the way he was, he could feel her pulse pounding and guessed she wasn't as unaffected by him as she pretended.

"You should know your father came to see me.''

She sighed. "What did he do this time?"

"He threatened me."

Distress was evident on her face. "Oh, J.P., I'm sorry. I'll talk to him. He's really harmless. I'll make him stop. Somehow," she said with a sigh.

"Good luck," he said with a laugh.

"Tell me about it. Especially now that he's got your mother as a willing accomplice. Fortunately, she's still an amateur." She looked up at him and caught her top lip between her teeth. "But if they—"

When she hesitated, he said, "I know their relationship is serious."

"How do you feel about that?"

"If he makes her happy, I'm okay with it. If he hurts her—"

"He won't." She touched his arm. "He's different now. His priorities have changed. He won't blow it. He knows Audrey's given him another chance at happiness."

"Second chances are a good thing," he said.

"I agree."

He slid his hands up and curved his fingers around her upper arms. "Does that mean I can hope that you'll give me a second chance?"

Her gaze searched his face. "I can't believe you'd want one. With me, I mean."

"Believe it."

Jordan's heart hammered so hard she felt as if she couldn't catch her breath. She was afraid to trust that everything she'd ever wanted was within her grasp. If she was dreaming, if he was joking, the hurting would be worse than before.

"After everything my father has done to you.... After everything you've been through...." She shook her head. "It's hard to believe you'd trust me. And without that, there's nothing."

His mouth thinned and a muscle jumped in his jaw. "This is going to sound crazy, but when I saw you on the road, one shoe off, walking in a circle, talking to yourself…" He shrugged. "I don't know. Something made me stop. I can't explain it, but it was almost as if some force caused me to pull over." He ran his fingers through his hair. "You think I'm nuts, don't you?"

"No." She stared at his wonderful face as hope blossomed inside her. "But I'll see your crazy story and raise you one. I was born on February 29."

"So your father said."

"So were my two best friends, in the same hospital. This year we celebrated our birthday in New Orleans. To make a long story short, we were in this weird little shop and the Gypsy gave us a lamp to rub and three wishes—one each."

"What was yours?"

"You may have noticed I can be sort of a smart aleck," she said.

A corner of his mouth turned up. "Yeah. I noticed."

"Well, I wished to be a princess and live in a palace." Jordan braced for his laughter.

He looked startled, but not call-the-men-in-the-white-coats startled. "No wonder you acted so funny—given where I live and what my middle name is."

"It's kind of a stretch," she admitted, "but there's enough substance to give one pause."

"Wow."

"Yeah, wow. But none of this has anything to do

with the trust issue. When you stopped on that road, I'd just been told that my hero would be there any minute to rescue me and I was supposed to fall in love with him.''

''Courtesy of your father.''

''Right. When you stopped, I was angrier than I've ever been in my life. And for the record, you were the one who gave me the idea. When I said I thought I was kidnapped, I was wondering whether or not it's technically kidnapping when arranged by one's own father. You said, and I quote, 'Can't you remember?' And I went with the idea. It was a gigantic misunderstanding, J.P.''

He shook his head. ''It was meant to be.''

''Do you believe that?''

''I fought it tooth and nail because of the circumstances.'' He smiled down at her. ''The truth is I'm glad our parents arranged this rendezvous. I've been miserable since that night you walked out. I'd have wasted a lot of time, but sooner or later, I'd have gone to you. You and I are meant to be together.''

''I feel it, too. I think I knew it almost from the beginning. But I couldn't understand how I could be attracted to a man my father chose. And I thought you were a workaholic just like him.''

He laughed. ''Perish the thought. Don't get me wrong—I love my work. But there are things that take priority.''

''I found that out. And when I did, I was a goner,'' she said.

He cupped her face in his hands. ''I love you, Jordan. Can you forgive me for being such a jerk?''

''There's nothing to forgive. I love you, too, J.P.''

''Will you marry me?''

"Yes," she said simply.

He let out a breath as he looked long and hard into her eyes. Then he lowered his head and touched his lips to hers. It felt so completely right. Jordan knew he sensed it, too.

When he broke off the kiss, she looked into his eyes. "When I marry Jonathan Prince Patterson, does that make me a princess?"

He smiled tenderly. "You will always be the ruler of my heart, the princess of my soul. And whether we live in a crate or a castle, as long as we're together, I'll be the happiest man on earth. I'm already the luckiest. It's not just any man who winds up with an heiress on his doorstep."

She smiled. "I can live with that."

Epilogue

When J.P. lovingly squeezed her hand, Jordan looked up at him and smiled. She'd been Mrs. Jonathan Prince Patterson for eight weeks, give or take a day. He had insisted they get married on New Year's Eve because he wanted to start the new year as husband and wife. Who was she to argue when she was head over heels in love?

Stopped at a traffic signal a block from Jackson Square, they waited for a walk sign. She glanced over her shoulder to see if their friends had caught up. Rachel and Jake Fletcher and Ashley and Max Caine had accompanied them on this birthday trip to New Orleans. The men were skeptical about the Gypsy/magic lamp/wish thing. The women wanted to show them the scene of the crime, so to speak.

When the other two couples finally joined them,

Jordan studied her redheaded friend. "What is it with you, Ash? Usually you're in the lead. Do you feel all right?"

Max Caine, her sandy-haired husband, looked at her with concern etched on his chiseled features. "I keep asking her the same thing, but she says she's fine."

"I am," Ashley protested. "Just a little tired."

Jordan could relate. She'd been feeling that way, too. Before she had time to comment, the other couple strolled to a stop beside her. "Hey, you two. Nice of you to join us."

Rachel leaned into her tall, handsome, brooding cowboy husband and his arm automatically went around her shoulders in a protective gesture. "It's so nice to be alone together," she said, smiling up at Jake.

Their nine-month-old daughter was at home with Cora Edens and Janie Compton, widowed sisters who lived together in Sweet Spring. Rachel had made friends with them when one was hospitalized where she used to work. Now Rachel was a full-time mom to Emma.

Jordan suspected that Rachel and Jake brought up the rear in this expedition, not because they were tired but because it was hard to walk fast while you gazed adoringly into each other's eyes.

"So where is this shop you wanted us to see?" Max asked.

"It's right around here somewhere," Ashley said, glancing up and down the street.

Tourists left over from Mardi Gras walked along, much like a year ago when the three of them had recovered the magic lamp. And after the exciting year they'd had, Jordan was convinced that lamp was filled to the brim with magic powers.

Rachel pointed. "Over there. That's where Jordan went toe to toe with that thug who stole the lamp."

Frowning, J.P. looked down at her. "You did what?"

"She's exaggerating," Jordan explained. "I tripped the guy, and he dropped the lamp then ran off. I picked it up and returned it to the Gypsy. The rest is magic."

"Magic," he said doubtfully. Her husband shook his head as he slid his arm around her waist, nestling her against him. "I wish you were a little more afraid. Do I need to get you a bodyguard to keep you in line?"

"No. All I need is your body to guard mine," she said, smiling up at him with just the right amount of wickedness. "And don't scoff. *Magic* is the operative word. If my father hadn't hired that chowderhead to kidnap me, we never would have met. He got that idea the night I retrieved the lamp." She shrugged. "You tell me it wasn't magic."

Ashley leaned her cheek against Max's shoulder. "I asked for money and power. Without my promotion at Caine Chocolate Company, I wouldn't have seen Max again. So on the magic issue, count me in on the believer side."

Rachel smiled up at Jake. "I wished for a baby, thinking courtship, love, marriage, children. But suddenly it was baby, oh baby. And Emma brought us together. I'll defend the magic factor to anyone who will listen."

Jordan stared up and down the street. "This is the right place. I'm sure of it. But I don't see the shop. It should be where that bookstore is."

Ashley tugged on Max's hand. "Let's go over there and ask."

They crossed at the light and checked out the bookstore in the same place where the shop had been. It was nothing like a year ago. No eerie green light. No fog. No Gypsy with a lamp. And the clerk they questioned said she knew nothing about the shop they described.

Back out on the sidewalk, Jordan noticed a fortune-telling machine resting against the brick wall. It was as tall as J.P. and inside the mechanical figure resembled Faith, their Gypsy, right down to the scarf covering her hair and the few black curls framing her face.

"Look at this," Jordan said. "Did anyone else see that *Twilight Zone* with the fortune-telling machine?"

Rachel shivered and Jake tightened his arm around her. "Now you're creeping me out." She frowned at the bizarre-looking thing. "But I have to confess. That night, for a split second when the light from inside was shining and she turned in the doorway, I thought she looked like June Cleaver."

Jordan figured that was pretty Freudian since Rachel had always wanted a traditional family. Now she had one with Jake.

Ashley glanced at Max then the rest of them. "The same thing happened to me, but I saw Hillary Clinton, a woman synonymous with money and power."

"Ditto for me," Jordan said. "Except I saw Princess Grace."

J.P. put his hand on her forehead, then looked at the other two men. "No fever."

She slugged him playfully. "We're not delusional. It really happened."

Rachel tapped her lip thoughtfully. "Remember that musical *Brigadoon* where the place only appeared once every hundred years? Maybe the shop is like that.''

"Could be,'' Ashley agreed. "Except it's here once every four years, for leap year.''

Jordan nodded. "And something about the three of us all being born on February 29 released the magic.''

Jake was checking out the fortune-telling machine. He put in a coin and the figure inside came to life. Lights started blinking. When the Gypsy's eyes popped open, the three women jumped back.

Then she spoke in a canned and very bad Hungarian accent. "Your daughter gives you great joy. When the time is right, you will be twice blessed with a son. There is much happiness ahead of you.''

When the machine shut off, Jake looked at Rachel. "The next baby is going to be a boy,'' she said happily.

He shook his head. "That's too weird.''

"Let me try it.'' Max pulled a coin from his pocket and slid it into the slot.

The same thing happened. When the Gypsy spoke she said, "Love is the sweetest of life's gifts. Soon yours will include a girl child with the woman of your dreams.''

Ashley's eyes widened. "I'm really creeped out now.'' She took Max's hand. "I haven't said anything because I wasn't sure. But I think I'm pregnant.''

"That's fantastic.'' He grinned broadly, then took her in his arms and lifted her off her feet, kissing her soundly.

After congratulations all around, everyone looked at Jordan and J.P. "What?'' he said.

"Your turn to take on the fortune-teller,'' Jake said.

Jordan fished a coin out of his pocket and wordlessly handed it to him.

"What if I don't want to know?"

She put her hands on her hips. "What if I do?"

"What part of no don't you understand?" he asked with a grin.

"The *N* and the *O*. So—no guts, no glory. Put the quarter in."

When he did, once again the mechanical Gypsy came to life. "In your princess you trust. She will soon give you a boy child to complete the circle of your love."

J.P. looked at her. "Are you pregnant?"

"I was going to do one of those test kits when we got home."

"Wow." A tender look swept into his eyes as he stared at her. Then he gently pulled her into his arms. "Okay. You win. I'm a believer."

"No, we win."

Thanks to three wishes. Rachel had a baby. Ashley had money and power, aka security. And Jordan had found her "prince." But they'd all learned love was the greatest gift of all. It truly was their hearts' desire.

* * * * *

If you enjoyed what you just read,
then we've got an offer you can't resist!

Take 2 bestselling
love stories FREE!

Plus get a FREE surprise gift!

////////////////////////////////

Clip this page and mail it to Silhouette Reader Service

IN U.S.A.	IN CANADA
3010 Walden Ave.	P.O. Box 609
P.O. Box 1867	Fort Erie, Ontario
Buffalo, N.Y. 14240-1867	L2A 5X3

YES! Please send me 2 free Silhouette Romance® novels and my free surprise gift. After receiving them, if I don't wish to receive anymore, I can return the shipping statement marked cancel. If I don't cancel, I will receive 6 brand-new novels every month, before they're available in stores! In the U.S.A., bill me at the bargain price of $21.34 per shipment plus 25¢ shipping and handling per book and applicable sales tax, if any*. In Canada, bill me at the bargain price of $24.68 plus 25¢ shipping and handling per book and applicable taxes**. That's the complete price and a savings of at least 10% off the cover prices—what a great deal! I understand that accepting the 2 free books and gift places me under no obligation ever to buy any books. I can always return a shipment and cancel at any time. Even if I never buy another book from Silhouette, the 2 free books and gift are mine to keep forever.

209 SDN DU9H
309 SDN DU9J

Name _____ (PLEASE PRINT)

Address _____ Apt.# _____

City _____ State/Prov. _____ Zip/Postal Code _____

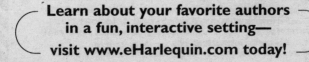

SILHOUETTE *Romance*®

COMING NEXT MONTH

#1714 THE PIED PIPER'S BRIDE—Myrna Mackenzie
The Brides of Red Rose

The women of Red Rose needed men—and they'd decided sexy Chicago bigwig Parker Monroe was going to help find them! But Parker wasn't interested in populating his hometown with eligible bachelors. Enter their secret weapon, Parker's former neighbor. But how was the love-shy Ellie Donahue supposed to entice her former crush to save the town without sacrificing her heart a second time?

#1715 THE LAST CRAWFORD BACHELOR—
Judy Christenberry
From the Circle K

Assistant District Attorney Michael Crawford was perfectly happy being the last unmarried Crawford son and he didn't need Daniele Langston messing it up. But when Dani aroused his protective instincts, his fetching co-*worker* became his co-*habitant*. Now this business-minded bachelor was thinking less about the courtroom and more about the bedroom....

#1716 DADDY'S LITTLE MEMENTO—Teresa Carpenter

The only convenient thing about Samantha Dell's marriage was her becoming a stepmother to precious eleven-month-old nephew Gabe. Living with Gabe's seductive reluctant daddy didn't work into her lifelong plans. *And getting pregnant by him?* Well, that certainly wasn't part of the arrangement! Would falling in love with her heartthrob husband be next?

#1717 BAREFOOT AND PREGNANT—Colleen Faulkner

Career-driven Ellie Montgomery had everything a girl could want—except a husband! But *The Husband Finder* was going to change that. Except, according to the book, her perfect match, former bad-boy Zane Keaton, was definitely Mr. Wrong! But a few of Zane's knee-weakening, heart-stopping kisses had Ellie wondering if he might be marriage material after all.

SRCNM0304